"Sandra Colbert's *Chicago Bound*, a collection of stories about the first generation immigrant experience in Chicago, was a pleasure to read. By turns charming, eloquent, or sad, each story was honed to a sharp edge, exposing an underlying darkness I didn't expect. Most are populated with ordinary individuals who may not recognize their flaws but deal with both joy and sorrow in a way that reinforces the humanity in us all. Colbert is definitely a writer to watch."

~Libby Fischer Hellmann
Author of *Nobody's Child*

"Sandra Colbert portrays working-class life in Chicago's Back of the Yards neighborhood in the immediate postwar era. Her stories tell the trials of young people growing up amidst the wooden frame tenements, packinghouses, and streets of a part of the city rarely visited by outsiders. With *Chicago Bound 2* she takes her place among Chicago's long line of realistic writers. The joy, grit, and heartbreak of the city make this collection especially vivid."

~Dominic A. Pacyga
Author of *Chicago: A Biography*

Reflections & Echoes

Also by the Author...

The Reason
(The First Book in the Kate Harrison Detective Series)

Dangerous Souls
(The Second Book in the Kate Harrison Detective Series)

Extradition
(The Third Book in the Kate Harrison Detective Series)

Chicago Bound

Chicago Bound 2: Time and Again

Reflections & Echoes

by Sandra M. Colbert

WINDY CITY
PUBLISHERS

Reflections & Echoes

Windy City Publishers
2118 Plum Grove Road, #349
Rolling Meadows, IL 60008
www.windycitypublishers.com

Published in the United States of America

ISBN:
978-1-953294-06-7

Library of Congress Control Number:
2021901586

Cover Image by Leigh Prather/Shutterstock.com

Windy City Publishers
Chicago

MEMORIES

"How sweet the silent backward tracings!
The wanderings as in dream—
the meditation of old times resumed—
their loves, joys, persons, voyages."

~Walt Whitman

Contents

 The Forgiving

My Dead Brother's Journal

"I'm so sorry that you lost your brother." Slathered my rosy, dumpling-cheeked co-worker. I didn't lose him, I wanted to bellow at the top of my lungs. I know exactly where he is. He's six feet under at the Veteran's Cemetery ninety miles from here. To lose something, is to imply that it can be found! You work for a magazine, sweet cheeks. Try to master the English language, Please!!

None of that, of course, was said. I nodded and calmly thanked her, as I've had to do dozens of times in the hours and days since IT happened.

IT being the unspeakable. IT being the new trajectory my life now took. IT being grief—the throes of grief and rage brought on by a little punk high on meth who went to a roadside mini- mart with a gun and began to shoot, killing my brother who had just hung up from talking to me, as he walked to the counter with his cup of Dr. Pepper. Poof! Alive and laughing one moment—dead the next. Not lost—dead! No other casualties, no one else in the place with even a scratch.

Just Mark—Sergeant Mark L. Wilder, U.S. Army, veteran of foreign wars, namely Afghanistan and Iraq. Age 29.

The little runt was easily found inside a nearby dumpster, quaking, and crying, led there by the tracks he left in the snow.

A Grief Counselor on hand at the magazine that I work for called me. She was probably glad that she suddenly had something to do. No mass shootings or tornadoes lately. No, I didn't want to make an appointment, I told her. But I politely listened. I can be polite. But a counselor—no. Hell, if you can't handle what life throws at you, you're a goner from the git-go.

Take off all the time that you need, use vacation days, she recommended.

And do what? I said, Think!

As it was, I went to work between IT happening and the funeral. Too soon? Didn't know what else to do. Had to keep busy.

You're a writer, she said. Keep a journal, it may help. Get it on paper. You need an outlet. That was my takeaway. Simple advice. So here I am keeping My Dead Brother's Journal, as I will call it. Innocuous, safe. A place where I can release all that I want to say and can't. Maybe I won't spew my real feelings to those grief free and smiling humans around me as I try to survive.

Is this an overstatement to say survival—to imply that my brother's death can destroy me? People lose loved ones every day, every hour, every minute. Why should this be any different? On a grief-o-meter, why is this at the top? Would it be any different if he took a bullet in Afghanistan? Or a car accident? Another question without an answer?

Yes, this is worse. Some crappy little stoner who should never have been born, took down my brother. Nothing noble here. Mark survived so much and to be taken down by this little shit defies all logic. Not that there is much logic in life. Too much randomness, too much chance, too much madness.

What no one seems to understand, what no one knows when they send flowers and cards and offer condolences, is just what my brother meant to me. It goes deeper then losing a sibling, which on its own, is a stupefying experience. I lost my best friend, my protector, my big brother, the go-to guy, the one that will always be there...or so I thought.

How do I do this thing, this life thing, by myself?

Maybe his death brings a summation of my life. Do I have to think about the unthinkable? The dregs of a wretched childhood surface—against my will.

Unmarried, not that it was ever a goal of mine. Most men bore me, good for the physical, and some laughs, not much more. As a result, no kids, thankfully. I'd make a lousy parent. No mom gene in me.

But I had lousy parents. Is lousy parenting hereditary? LOL, the current lexicon for laughter.

The Crux of the Problem? Of all my problems? No, can't be. I shed them like a thrashed, flea-infested winter coat. Of course, I did.

My rage is not only homed in on the meth head shooter, but on them—Judy and Joe, my parents, never mom and dad.

Me—an accident. I was told more than once during one of dear mother's drunken tirades. A pain in the ass. Not like Mark—the firstborn, the pride and joy, the best and brightest. Did I resent him?

No, never. Because he was all that they said he was, and more. He was my protector on those Saturday nights when they came staggering into our doublewide trailer after a night of drinking at the nearby bar. We knew to stay out of the way. They would fight their way through some unintelligible argument until one or the other, usually my mother, would turn their drunken rage on us, or it seemed, on me. I knew when to hide.

Their tirades usually ended up with sex.

When I was young, really young, I would cry in fear when I heard the guttural sounds coming from the other side of the cheap, thin walls of the doublewide. Thunder and lightning had nothing on the howling noises my mother could make, not to mention the grunts coming from my father. Mark would turn up the radio to drown out the obscene wails and yelps. We would sing along with the songs or he would tell me stories until the two of them finally passed out.

My mother worked at a nearby hardware store. My father a construction worker of some kind. He seemed to be laid off more than employed. Money was the catalyst for most fights and the reason that food and new clothing was sporadic.

It was Mark who made sure I was dressed and fed before going to school, while the two of them slept. He was a good cook at an early age. It was Mark who helped with homework and brought home books for me from the library. It was Mark, who blocked the slaps that seemed to come on so easily and unexpectedly.

It was Mark who walked me to school and kept an eye on me in high school. It was Mark that I confided in when I liked a boy or if the girls were mean to me, as adolescent girls can be.

It was Mark that protected me. It was Mark who played the role of parent.

When he turned eighteen, he enlisted in the Army. For the first and only time in my life, I do believe I was hysterical. How could you? I screamed. You can't leave me with them! I cried. Don't go! I selfishly begged.

I need a life. I can't stay here. He yelled back. I have to get out and get out far away. You'll be eighteen in a couple of years. You can take off then. You're smart. You can go to community college, maybe the big college in Chicago. You'll be fine. You're tough.

You'll be fine.

He was right. I survived, but I left before I turned eighteen with one of the girls in town who was moving to Chicago. I graduated early because I was in an advanced class. Left a note and took off. After I was settled, I never even gave them my address. Mark said that wasn't right. I didn't care. I never wanted to see either one of them again, I told him.

And I didn't...until the funeral.

Part two—they are a part of my rage. Aside from the mutant that did the shooting, my parents are the reason that Mark was where he was that day. He visited them when he was home on leave and when he was no longer in the service, he would go every couple of months and for Christmas.

Mark was big on duty. Be it duty to our country or duty to our parents. That day he was there to give them money. My father declaring that he was too banged up to work and couldn't get unemployment money anymore and was too young for social security. Good old Mark was there to help them out...again.

He was on his way home when he stopped for gas and a soda. After filling me in on the visit with some good laughs, it was then that he ended up on the dirty floor of the mini mart with a bullet in his chest.

I feel that my whole being, my very soul is being devoured by hatred and pain. Will there be anything left of the person who existed before IT happened?

~~~~~~

"Mi pequeño Esteban, Mi pequeño Esteban"

Steven could hear her voice as clearly as if she were standing next to him in the grimy cell.

"Mama, Mama," he wept, a rivulet of tears splashed on his orange jumpsuit. "Why did you have to leave me? Why did you have to die? I need you, Mama. I need you. I'm so scared."

The vomiting from the withdrawal stopped but the nausea and shakes hadn't. The heart palpitations still came along with the sweating. Steven had never felt as sick as he had these last few days. He was given medication and told it would help. He didn't want it to help. He wanted to suffer. He knew he deserved to suffer.

The arraignment ended hours before, the jail cell door slamming once again behind him, leaving him even more bewildered and frightened.

The sight of his father, as he wiped away tears of his own, and who tried to reassure him that everything would be all right, just made it all worse. His grandmother and aunt stood next to his father. They looked as dazed as they did on the day of his mother's funeral.

"How could this have happened? You're a good boy. What went wrong? How could this happen?" He could hear them despite their muteness.

I don't know! he wanted to scream. I don't know!

But he did know. It was the guys at school. Looking back, he couldn't remember their names. In his mind they were "The Guys". They seemed to come out of nowhere. They gravitated toward him when he started skipping classes—skipping classes because it all seemed so irrelevant when you watched your mother, the person that meant everything to you, die a tortuous death. Irrelevant when your grieving father fled into his job and left you with relatives. Left unsaid, but he knew the sight of him, the resemblance to his mother, was the reason his father stayed away.

He let grief make him invisible.

It was the guys who came up with something to help him cope. Something that made him laugh again, made him forget. It worked... at times.

But it was expensive. Pilfering cash from his father and grand-mother didn't begin to cover the price of a few good hits. The need for it increased. The desire for it magnified.

Steven couldn't remember when someone put the gun in his hand. It started out as a drive out to the country with the guys. He could remember the cravings, the need creeping up on him. The shakes, the sweats had already started. He had to get the money.

Just show them the gun, someone said. They'll give you the cash. We'll wait right here. Make it fast. Then someone put the gun in his sweaty hand. Go! Now! Someone ordered.

He held out the gun to the man behind the counter with shaking hands and ordered him to hand over the money. It was like a scene in a movie that he was suddenly transported into.

He saw the man coming with the soda cup in his hand. A big guy. He looked tough. This guy could see what was happening and would try to stop him.

Steven had to do something.

The gunshot thundered. The blood a violent crimson. But it was the look of complete shock on the man's face as he fell that would stay with Steven forever. The dying seconds that asked "why?"

The arraignment was a continuation of the nightmare. The words from the cops, the lawyers, a blur of words and phrases. The victim, former soldier, a hero, an innocent bystander forever felled by the actions this killer, yes, a teenager, but a killer, a murderer.

Steven had no idea who was speaking. It didn't matter. He wanted to die. He wanted to be with his mother.

My Dead Brother's Journal, continued

The funeral. No wake, just a dignified military funeral. I made a point of NOT acknowledging Joe and Judy. I stood opposite them at the gravesite. Mark's two best friends at my side holding my arms, as if I would collapse. Truth be told, I almost did when Taps was being so mournfully played. Mark would have liked it. So many people, mostly military. Because Mark wasn't married, the flag was given to Judy. I closed my eyes, but I could hear her theatrical wail. I wondered if she was sober.

I love the symmetry of a military cemetery. The white headstones, the precisely carved names and dates, the abstract purity. So peaceful.

I didn't want to leave. I wanted to stay with my brother. I had so much that I wanted to tell him. Someone kept tugging at my arm, telling me that it was time to go. But I'll come back, I vowed—every chance I get. I have to make sure everything is right with his grave. I'll bring little flags, maybe flowers. Though he wasn't a flower guy.

The arraignment is tomorrow. I get to see the loathsome animal that did this. He'll pay for this—bigtime.

Greg couldn't stop the nervous gestures—the foot tapping, the quiver of his hands. This was foreign territory; more foreign than any country he had ever visited.

He had been in traffic court twice in his lifetime, but this wasn't anything like traffic court. This was raucous, disorderly, harsh.

He was sitting in the front row with his mother and sister. His mother playing with her purse handle. Her expression reflected her fears. His sister, stoic as usual—ready to take charge.

For Greg, the overwhelming guilt ate at him. He failed. He failed his wife, his family and most of all—his son. He let grief devour him. There was no room left for his son.

It happened so fast. It started with a headache that wouldn't go away. She finally went to the doctor, had tests done. Brain tumor. She died three weeks later. A month of disorientation and pain. He watched as she, in a drug induced state, no longer knew her son or her husband. She died in his arms with her weeping son at her side.

The nightmare didn't end there. It continued with the call that came in just after he landed. Almost unintelligible jabber from his mother saying that Steven was arrested—arrested for murder. The thought that his mother was suffering some sort of stroke was his first thought, his brain refusing to accept what she was saying.

How can it happen? He asked himself so many times. How did it go from a life with a beautiful wife, a smart and happy son to becoming a widower with a drug addled son accused of murder?

Marty scanned the court room, annoyed that it was so crowded and chaotic.

She sat in the front row behind the prosecutors' table. It was important to get a good look at the person who killed her brother.

She stiffened when she heard a voice from the back of the court room. It was her father's, probably with her mother in tow. She closed her eyes. *How can this go from bad to worse?* she thought.

She studied the section behind the defense attorney's table. A muddle of individuals—men and women, mostly different shades of brown and white, all indistinct. She wondered which ones were part of the killer's family. A tall blond in the first row stood out, flanked by two white women.

Her brother's killer's name was called out. A kinetic charge ran through her body. She felt her stomach clench.

Steven Soto Hammond—a name she associated with evil.

He shuffled in, his head down, grimy, dark hair covering his face. He looked up at the people gathered behind the defense attorney's table. Marty could see the fear in his dark eyes. She could almost smell it on him. It was palpable. There wasn't any of the cockiness that she expected. He was young—too young to have killed someone. This must be a mistake. Maybe it wasn't him.

The attorney did the talking. When the boy did speak, the judge told him to speak louder.

He repeated "not guilty". Marty heard her father scream "bullshit" from the back of the room.

A few more words exchanged—bail set at two hundred thousand dollars. More words exchanged about his age. The attorneys arguing about whether he should be tried as an adult. That was when she heard the age. Sixteen. *Old enough to know better,* Marty thought. *Try him as an adult. Too bad there is no death penalty.*

Then it was over.

She watched as he turned toward the people in the first row. The blond man stood and tried to reach out to him, muttering how everything would be all right. He would see him in a little while.

Who was this blond man, she wondered? Foster parent, social worker? Some too-soft-hearted public servant ready to make excuses for the little monster.

Marty watched as he left his seat followed by the two women. She followed close behind.

After they walked through the doors, he stopped to say something to the two women. They went in one direction. He watched them as they walked away.

Marty approached him and asked,

"So, who are you to him?"

"Pardon me?"

"The Hammond punk. What are you to him? Social worker, foster parent, what?"

The man slowly reddened as he looked at Marty.

"Who are you? What do you want?" he asked, defensively.

"Who am I?" she countered. "Marty Wilder. That's who am I? I'm the sister of the man that was murdered by that little monster."

The man covered his face, then looked away for a moment before he spoke.

"I'm his father."

"His what?" she replied.

"I know. No resemblance. His mother was Spanish, from Barcelona. He took after her side."

Marty gaped at the tall blond; all her prearranged comments left unsaid.

"I don't know what to say," he said. "Saying sorry can't begin to cover it. I can't imagine what you and your family are going through."

"You're right. You can't."

"I know it's an awful time—it's horrible," he continued. "I wish there was something I could say. But he's a good kid. He made some bad choices. He's my boy and I love him. And he did something terrible."

"Bad choices?" Marty snapped. "Bad choices. My brother is dead because of his bad choices."

He looked away.

"Where's his mother?" she continued, her voice still tinged with anger.

"She died. Almost six months ago. He took it really bad. They were close. He ended up doing drugs to cope with the grief, I guess, and then this happened."

Marty felt sudden pulsing in her ears.

"Where the hell were you?" she asked, holding on to the anger.

"Listen, I can't talk about it, not here, not now. I have to go see him. Like I said, saying I'm sorry doesn't cut it, but I don't know what else to say."

"I want that kid of yours to spend the rest of his life in jail."

"I'm sure you do, and I understand how you can feel that way, but..."

"No, no "but". You failed. You failed as a father. Now your kid is a murderer."

"Don't you think I know that" he replied, his voice taking on a quiver and rising. "It's a nightmare. It's a god-awful fucking nightmare for all of us."

"I don't want to hear about it," she interrupted. "I don't want to hear another god-damn word."

She turned and nearly sprinted away. The need to scream or cry greater than ever.

It was when she neared the exit doors that she heard her name being called. She didn't have to turn around to know that it was her father's voice.

"Martha." She heard him say in a voice that he used on her as a child, whenever she disobeyed or defied him.

She stopped and turned to face them. Her father was stomping toward her with her mother lagging behind.

"What?"

"What? What? Is that all you have to say to us? After all this time. You snubbed us at the funeral and now this."

Her mother now stood behind her husband, clutching a tissue, her face marked with anxiety.

"And you expected what. Some family reunion. Hugs and kisses."

"We raised you better than this."

"You never raised me. Mark raised me. You two were too busy thinking about yourselves, your next party, your next drink, coping with your latest hangover to give two shits about us."

"That's not true," her mother whimpered. "That's just not true."

"Don't you think that we're suffering, girl," her father said. "We lost our boy. Our son. No parents should bury their child. Not natural. And not like this."

"Listen," she said. "I don't know what you want from me. If it's money, you're not getting it from me. I'm not Mark. You're on your own."

Her mother let out a sob.

"That's cruel," her father said. "We don't deserve that. Your mother don't deserve that. How'd we ever end up with such a cruel, mean, bitch for a daughter..."

Her mother pulled her husband's arm, his face red with rage.

"Let's go, Joe. She don't want nothing to do with us. Let's just go. I can't take no more."

Marty stepped aside and watched them hurriedly walk past her and out the double doors.

My Dead Brother's Journal, continued

Back to my Dead Brother's Journal with a glass of vodka this time. The Xanax isn't cutting it. I need something stronger to get me through this new version of hell.

The father—god damn. So, he's not some gang banger, undocumented thug from across the border. A kid, a scrawny, pimply faced kid. Go figure. Still a killer.

And Joe and Judy. All a bit much for one day.

Cruel—He called me cruel. I'm not cruel. I have friends, although I haven't seen them much lately. I know they wouldn't call me cruel.

This is about justice. I see so much lack of justice. I write for a magazine. I read two papers a day. I listen to NPR. And it keeps happening. People literally getting away with murder, with child abuse, with spousal abuse, with every damn crime in the books. Smart lawyers for the rich and payoffs for the politicians.

I won't let that happen here. The kid must pay for what he did. Yes, he goes to jail, for a very, very, long time. He gets out as an old man some day for good behavior. My brother never got to see another day. My brother will never grow old.

This is about justice—good old fashion justice.

And my parents—well they blew their chance with me. If they had acted like decent parents, I wouldn't feel this way. They're older now—and of course, they won't face up to what they did in the past. It's all about denial. Well, I haven't forgotten. Why should I?

I'm not cruel. Things have to be made right. I'm tired and I want to talk to Mark. He would understand.

Marty tried to concentrate on her work. It took more of an effort than ever before. The vodka hangovers were happening more often.

The sound of her phone ringing made matters worse. As she reached to answer it, she prayed that it wasn't a problem call. The thought of putting out any fires this morning seemed beyond her.

Seconds passed before the name and voice registered. It was Frank Nichols, the prosecuting attorney handling the case.

"The father wants to have a sit down with you." he told her.

"What?"

"Yeah, he wants to meet with you and just talk."

"What do we have to talk about? His kid killed my brother."

"In cases like this, the family is allowed to speak before the sentence is laid down. Maybe he's hoping you'll tell the world, the judge that is, that all is forgiven and go easy on the kid."

"You're kidding."

"Nope. It works most of the time in either direction. Sometimes, depending on what the family members say, the sentencing can be lenient or really harsh."

"You think he wants me to go easy on his kid."

"That's my guess."

"No way. Fat chance."

"I had a feeling that's what you would say. But I have his number in case you decide that you do want to meet him. Write this down."

Without thinking, she grabbed a pen and took down the number.

"I'm not doing this."

"You don't have to. It's entirely up to you."

"Well, I won't."

"So, don't. I have to go," he said. "I have the fate of other innocents in my hands. If you change your mind and do meet him, let me know. I'm just being curious here."

"Yeah, okay."

She slammed the phone down and reached for the aspirins in her purse. Her shaking hands made it difficult to open the container. The urge to cry once again overtook her. Cursing, she threw the pills against the wall.

My Dead Brother's Journal, continued

I hate not being in control. I've always been in control. Big emotional scenes turn my stomach. I have to curb the vodka when I get home. I have to get a grip. I lost it at work today. Too many heads turned today. I actually ran from my desk in tears.

I had to put up with my co-workers asking me if I was alright.

What could that punk's father want to talk to me about? Leniency? Does he want to brag about what a great kid his son is? Why? To what end?

Why can't I stop thinking about it? Why does this bother me so much? I wish Frank never called me. I should just toss the number and be done with it.

But I'm curious. It's going to eat at me. I need a drink. I need to sleep—a dreamless sleep. Mark comes to me in my dreams. He looks and sounds so real. I'm a little girl in the dreams and he's a grown man. He makes me laugh. I can hear his voice. I try so hard not to wake up. Some nights, he's angry with me and I don't know why.

It was up to me to clean out his apartment. I went there with two of his friends. Fortunately, my brother was a minimalist. Not much in the way of non-essentials in his apartment. That may have come from all those years in the military. I gave away what I could to his two buddies and the rest to Goodwill and the dumpster. I tried not to think as I made all his possessions disposable. I came home with his books and boxes of pictures, cards and letters. There was the military paraphernalia too. His friend Scott said that maybe some of the military stuff should go to my parents. I told him to take care of it. He said he will. Some day when I feel I could handle it I'll go through the boxes. Not now.

Another weekend coming up. Those are the worst. Not enough to keep me busy.

Marty stood at her twentieth-floor apartment window and looked down on the city. A great view of the lake and the skyline—the one place where she always wanted to be when not working. Mark was impressed that she had that kind of money. Hey, it's my big extravagance, she would tell him. I work my butt off for this place. I love it here.

Nothing could quell the restlessness that dogged her that Saturday morning. The four-mile run that she took earlier left her sore. The breakfast at her favorite café left her nauseous. The nice weather irritated her.

Four o'clock. She was going to meet him in four hours. She told herself that this was the only way to get past this. It was curiosity—pure and simple. Curiosity. She would hear him out. Get it out of her system and come back home. A vodka cocktail would be her reward for tackling this head on and getting it over with.

She was abrupt and all business when she called him. He said little. He told her she could name the place. She did. He named the time. She agreed.

Now standing and looking out at the clouds gathering over the lake, she wished it had been over coffee at a café. It would be over by now.

It was a trendy modern bar with the windows facing Michigan Avenue. She took a seat facing the avenue. She got there early. She had her drink in front of her and paid for before he got there. He walked in at four o'clock exactly. *Must be his pilot training to be at place at the exact time that was assigned*, she thought.

He spotted her and walked over. He gave a small smile. She nodded.

"Thank you for coming," he started.

"Yeah. So, what is it that you want?" she replied.

"Ah, I thought I'd order a drink first," he said, annoyed by her abruptness. "Is that okay?"

Nothing was said as they waited for staff to take his beer order.

"I thought it would be a good for us to meet and not be at the court-house. Neutral ground, so to speak."

She took a drink and glared at him.

"I don't know why I agreed to this," she said. "Or why you would want to meet with me."

"I'm not sure myself. It just seems that we should. It's important."

"It is? Or are you just hoping I'll beg for leniency for your kid. You know. Forgive and forget. Kids—whadya going to do with them?"

His beer arrived and he took a drink before replying.

"I want to hear about your brother, and I want you to hear about my son."

"Not a conversation that I want to be a part of. No thanks. Anything else?"

"Listen, we are both going through something incredibly awful. Our lives will never be the same. But I think, I just think..."

"You think what? Getting this all out and put into words will make it all so much easier."

He shrugged.

"Wrong," she said. "So wrong. The more we know the worse it will be. Oh, and please don't tell me that you're some kind of holy roller and God will make it all better. Maybe we should pray together? That's not likely to happen either."

"No, that's the last thing I want to do. I'm trying to find the best way to deal with this. Maybe without the hostility. I'm hoping you can get past the all-out hatred that you feel for my son right now."

"Not likely. You have no idea what I'm going through."

"And you have no idea of what I'm going through and what Steven is going through. Or my mother and the rest of our family. It's been a hell that I don't think I can ever put into words."

She looked out the window and watched the street bustling with tourists and shoppers, wishing she were one of them.

"I also wanted you to hear this from me," he added.

"Hear what?"

"Steven is out on bail."

"Hmm. That must of cost you a tidy cent."

"It did. It cost everything I have and plus some. But I couldn't let him stay in that god-awful hell hole of a jail with thugs who, who..."

"Yeah, I get it. You don't have to paint a picture," she replied with a smirk. "So, he's safe and sound at home watching movies and playing video games."

"Not exactly. There is someone with him every second. Even sleeping in his room with him. We're terrified that he'll commit suicide. He's mentioned it more than once. He cries very easily, and it takes a lot of effort to get him to eat. And when he does, it doesn't always stay down. He's skin and bones."

Again, Marty turned her attention to the people passing by.

"There are death threats on-line. My brother-in-law is a cop, and he spends a lot of time at our place. I don't own a gun. I don't want one in my house, but I may be forced to get one."

Marty's only response was to order another drink.

"Tell me about your brother." Greg said after the drink came.

"Why?"

"I don't know. I just think," he hesitated. "I feel like I should know everything, no matter how awful or how hard it would be to hear. How much worse can it get? I don't want any surprises. I need to deal with everything head on, not just for me but for Steven."

It was after the drink came that Marty responded.

She spoke so softly that Greg struggled to hear her. Her eyes that had been so filled with anger now took on a vacant look.

"He was all I really had. He was my big brother, the one that took care of me when my parents fell short. Actually, he was the one that took care of me when the world fell short. He was everything to me."

She took a drink and looked at him.

"Have you ever lost a sibling?" she asked.

"No. It's just me and my sister."

"Losing a sibling, in itself, is a unique loss. It's that connection to the past—that shared history, the good, the bad, the giggles, the tears. There's a void in your life, actually more like a hole—a huge gaping hole. Then sometimes it's like there's this object in front of you. It's something real. You reach out to grab it and then it turns to dust. Sometimes it's too painful to remember the past and the good times that you shared. So, you force yourself to stop remembering."

Greg didn't respond. He could read the pain in her eyes.

"And that's all I have to say, other than I'm out of here. I don't think we have anything else to talk about."

"That's not true. I think we have a lot to talk about," he answered.

She finished off her drink and grabbed her purse.

"No, no we don't. I'll see you in court."

"Marty," he called after her.

"What?"

"Call me if you want to tell me more or if you want to know more."

"I don't see that happening," she replied. She turned and walked away.

Moments later he watched as she merged with the crush of people on Michigan Avenue.

My Dead Brother's Journal, continued

I meant it when I said I don't see that happening. He doesn't get it. NO ONE DOES!

Some things can't be put into words.

I've once heard that the worst part of losing someone is that when you look to the future you realize that you have to go through life without that person.

I guess that's what this kid has to live with—losing his mother at such an early age. And then this.

And his father, probably still trying to come to grips with losing his wife.

I'm not a cruel person. I feel sorry for them.

But look at what I have to deal with now.

Marty called Frank that following Monday morning.

"I met him for a drink. He told me about his kid, and he asked me about Mark. I told him a little. I can't remember all of what I said. And then I left. No big deal."

"It is kind of a big deal. The trial is in a few weeks. Like I told you earlier, a statement from you can carry some weight. Do you think he's pressuring you to say something favoring his son?"

"I didn't get that impression. I'm really not sure what he wanted from me. He said he needed to know everything no matter how hard it would be to handle."

She heard him grunt at the other end.

"He told me the kid is suicidal," she told him.

"Really? Not surprising. Teenagers tend to be suicidal at that age to begin with. Hope it doesn't happen. I doubt that he'll get life. He could still have a future."

"And there are death threats."

"When aren't there death threats?" he replied. "In this day and age, everyone thinks that they're avengers. Truth and justice and the American way. Blah, Blah. Most of the time, it's just sick rants from pimply-faced cowards."

"And sometimes, it's not. Right?"

"Right. But hell, if you saw my emails after some of these cases, half the population of the state wants me dead. It passes with time. I'm still here. I don't know of any dead prosecutors...so far."

"Well, I don't plan on having any more meetings with him," Marty said. "It was tough on me and probably tougher on him. I don't really understand why he wants to put himself through more hell."

"Everyone handles these things differently. He's a smart man. He needs to know all the facts. Some people are just like that. Others would rather bury their heads in the sand and ignore the facts. The facts can get in the way of the rage that they feel. They want to carry that rage with them until the day they die. I think they feel they owe it to the person that they lost."

"Frank?"

"Yeah."

"Never mind. I've got to get back to work."

"Okay. Keep in touch."

"Yeah. I will," she said as she ended the call.

My Dead Brother's Journal, continued

Mark's lawyer has been in touch. So has his insurance company. I've been bad about returning their calls. Whatever they have to say just makes it all the more real. I don't want to profit from this.

I finally called them back. Mark didn't have too much in his savings, by some standards. He left most of it to me. Some contributions to some VA charities. The rest to me. Not to my parents. I guess, when he drew up the will, which he did before he went to the Middle East, he probably figured they would just piss it all away on booze and casino gambling.

The insurance company has a sizable amount that he also left to me. I'm putting it in a savings account. I don't know what else to do with it. Maybe someday it'll come in handy, like when I need a nursing home. I can't imagine having a good time with it.

The conversations with these people are tearing me apart. I wish he would have left it all to charity. The fact that he wanted to take care of me after he was gone...

Frank's words keep cropping up. I try to shove them away but can't. Am I one of those that want to carry this rage with me until the end of my days? What if the kid commits suicide? How would I feel? Would I be glad?

I'm not a cruel person.

~~~~~~

Marty literally tripped over one of the Mark's boxes in her foyer. She had set them in her foyer when she brought them back from his apartment. They were still there, unopened.

After she righted herself, she stood in the foyer staring down at them as if they were foreign objects that found their way into her apartment.

She hauled them up and put them in the living room and continued to stare at them.

With a sigh and trembling hands she opened the smallest box.

My Dead Brother's Journal, *continued*

I finally opened one of Mark's boxes. The smallest one—the ones with cards and letters. I didn't realize that he saved so much correspondence. I guess he was always a sentimental slob. But I'm glad that I saved his letters and printed out some of his e-mails. Someday, when I think I can cope, I'll read a few. Maybe someday, if I ever have kids, at this rate not too likely, I'll tell them about their Uncle Mark and what a great guy he was, and I'll read his letters. Maybe someday.

He saved every birthday card he ever got. What a pack rat! The funniest and the dirtiest of course, are from me. I heard myself laugh when I read them. Can't remember the last time I laughed.

He had a lot of girlfriends. Some I remember. Some I never heard of. He did get around. A lot of them were at the funeral. They got to meet each other there. That would crack him up.

I wonder if there is some kind of an afterlife. Do spirits really hang around? I once heard that if you died abruptly, like he did, the spirit remains for a while. We're basically electrical impulses and that electrical energy keeps on going even though the body stopped. That's why there are ghosts and unexplained events. I'd like to think that Mark is floating around somewhere still looking out for me. I wish he'd give me a sign.

The cards from my parents—there's a lot of them. All in my mother's handwriting.

"We're so proud of you." That's how she ended every letter and birthday card. Not "love" but "We're so proud of you." Their birthday cards are large and flowery, sentimental, and poetic. On one of the cards—his last birthday card—she actually wrote that she was sorry for not being a better mother. "We lost Martha because of not being such good parents. I'm sorry that she wants nothing to do with us. I'm proud of her too. Maybe someday, we can get her back. We're better now. Maybe age does that."

Marty had to control the urge to throw the box across the room. Instead, she gripped it until the cardboard split.

"Mark!" she screamed to the empty room. "Dammit Mark, I need to talk to you! Where the fuck are you? I can't handle any of this. I'm not like you. I can't handle this kind of stuff."

She let the tears swallow her up.

Once spent, she went to the kitchen and her bottle of vodka.

It was after a couple of drinks that she dialed the number.

"Can you meet me later?" she hoped that her speech wasn't slurred.

"I'm at the airport. I'm off tomorrow. Where do you want to meet?"

"At Grant Park. Find a bench. I'll find you. At about 11:00."

"Fine. I'll bring coffee."

"Tea. Chai tea."

"Okay. Chai tea at 11:00.

My Dead Brother's Journal, continued

Damn vodka. I'm still not sure why I called him.

Mark's box of letters and cards triggered something—not sure what.

There were pictures. Pictures with kids. He coached a little league team. I vaguely remember that. There's a picture that someone took-it's obviously somewhere in the Middle East. He's surrounded by about a dozen bedraggled kids. Their clothes are barely hanging on to their skinny bodies. But they're smiling. They're standing around my brother and smiling, maybe even laughing. He's got this broad smile on his face—like he's enjoying this. God, I wish I knew the back story on this. I may have to contact a couple of his army friends. They might know.

I'm getting annoyed with him. Doesn't he ever stop being a saint?

It was a clear, sunny day. The kind of day that sometimes feels like it will never come during the dismal Chicago weather.

Greg was on a bench, the two containers next to him. She approached him slowly.

"Hi," she murmured.

She could see the dark rims around his eyes. He looked thinner, sadder.

"Hi," he replied, glancing up at her. "Here's your tea. They put milk in it. Hope that's okay."

"Yeah, it's fine. That's how I take it."

Neither spoke while they both sipped their drinks.

"Nice out today," she finally said.

"Yes. Yes, it is."

"We don't get so many picture-perfect days like this."

"No, no we don't," he replied. "But we're not here to discuss the weather. Could you tell me why we're here?"

"How's your son doing?"

"Steven is hanging on—just barely but hanging on. The closer we get to the court date, well, the worse it's for all of us," he said. "You could have asked me that on the phone, so, once again, why are we here?"

"To be perfectly honest, I'm not quite sure myself."

"I went through some of Mark's things yesterday," she said after a long pause. "It dawned on me how much he liked kids. He was always coaching little league teams and when he was still in the service, he would speak at some of the local high schools. He was good with kids. So, this is even more of a punch in the gut."

"Is this supposed to make me feel better," he replied not hiding his anger. "You want me to let Steven know that he killed someone who would have been a buddy? Aren't we going through enough?"

"No, don't misunderstand. I, I.,"

"You what?"

"You said you wanted to know about Mark, so I'm telling you. I couldn't the last time that we met. But when I saw those pictures, I saw the opposite of me. I saw a person who wouldn't be raging at the world. Instead, he would have tried to understand what happened. If this happened to me, I really think he would have grieved for the killer's family as much as for me. He saw so much death and suffering in the Middle East, but I have a picture of him smiling and surrounded by a group of kids and they're smiling too. How does that happen in a war-torn country?" "What have they got to smile about?" she continued. "Those kids were probably orphans who've seen things that we can't even imagine, but he's got them smiling."

"He never brought the war home with him. He hardly spoke about it. And I, somewhat selfishly because I didn't want to know, well, I never asked about it. I made jokes and told him my troubles instead."

"He sounds like a hell of a guy. Most GI's are like that," Greg replied. "You're right. I did say I wanted to know, but now I'm not so sure. I don't know just how much more I can take. I'm trying to stay strong for Steven and I don't think I'm doing such a great job.

"I have to keep on working," he continued. "God knows I need the money, but I need to be with him as well. I wasn't there for him when his mother died and that's why this happened. It's on me. It's something I have to live with. Maybe that's why I want to know about Mark. Maybe it's a form of self-flagellation. You want to punish my son. I want to punish myself."

She waited until she could find the words before she responded.

"Tell me about your wife."

Greg looked over at her.

"Please," she said. "How did she die? What happened?"

"What happened? A brain tumor happened. One day she was a beautiful, brilliant archeologist, a great mother. The next she was a withered, suffering shell of the woman that she once was. It happened fast.

Headaches, dizzy spells, the tests, the diagnosis, then a few weeks later, the end. I told myself that was a blessing. The pain, the loss of her functions, the drugs that kept the pain away, but left her almost comatose. Towards the end, I'm not sure if she even recognized any of us. I hope she did."

"I'm sorry."

"Yeah, so am I. And I'm sorry about your brother. I'm sure I would have liked him."

"Everyone liked him," Marty said. "Me, I'm the brittle angry one. I'm the ambitious one who's going to show the world how great I am because I overcame a lousy childhood."

"How did you meet her?" she asked.

"What?"

"How did you meet your wife?"

"I fly international. It was when I was on a layover in Barcelona. Like I said, she was an archeologist, a good one. She was at a restaurant in the airport waiting for a flight to the US for a conference on the latest findings at Pompei. Turned out she was going to be on my flight to Chicago.

"God, she was beautiful. And so freaking smart. She spoke English probably better than me. It happened fast. We were married seven months later. Steven came a year later. The happiest time in my life. I didn't think anyone could be happier."

To anyone walking by, they looked like a couple comfortable in their silence, drinking from their Starbucks cups and enjoying the day out.

The silence between them lingered.

Greg stood and looked around.

"It's my turn to get up and walk away," he said as he stood to go. "I guess I'll see you in court."

"Wait. Don't go yet."

"Why not? I'm tired and I really don't feel much like continuing this conversation. You were right. What you said the last time me met. You were right."

"What was that?"

"You said, the more we know the worse it will be. You were right. I just want to get through this, and I don't want my son to suffer any more then he already has."

"I'll ask for leniency."

"What?"

"The judge will let someone from the family speak. They can do that. I'll...I'll ask them to go easy on him. I'll ask for leniency."

"You'd do that?"

"Yeah. I can't take much more either. I'm sick of all the pain. And besides, I do believe that Mark would want that. If he survived the gunshot, he would have asked the court to go easy. Hell, he probably would have met with you and Steven. He was like that. I'm the vengeful one. He wasn't."

"I don't know what to say."

"Tell Steven that. Tell him it's going to be alright. Tell him, well just tell him to hang in there. He'll come out of this in one piece."

"Okay. I will. Thank you."

"Yeah, well. You don't have to thank me. I better let you go. I'll see you in court."

My Dead Brother's Journal, continued

I don't know if I said that to make him feel better or to make me feel better about myself.

Maybe this is just another way that Mark is taking care of me. I can grieve but I have to shake the rage. I have to move on from this wretched anger. I guess in a way he's teaching me something.

Marty's parents were in the front row, behind the prosecutors table. The seat next to them was empty. She sat next to her mother. No words were exchanged. Her mother reached over, almost timidly and squeezed Marty's hand. Marty didn't pull back.

She looked over the aisle and saw Greg with his mother and sister. All three looked defeated, sadness etched on their faces.

Greg looked over at her. He gave her a slight nod and wave. She nodded and gave a slim smile back.

She caught her breath when Steven was escorted in the courtroom. He looked even younger and smaller. The suit he wore looked two sizes too large, almost like a Halloween costume. His eyes carried such a look of fear that Marty thought if he could run, he would, just out of sheer terror.

His grandmother held out her empty arms. The realization that she was forbidden to touch him all the more obvious and painful.

Marty watched as his attorney spoke to him. The boy nodded mutely. Greg leaned forward to send a few words. The boy made a short reply.

The trial turned out to be even more brutal than Marty anticipated. The details of her brother's last minutes were spelled out in agonizing details by the witnesses and the officers on the scene. She heard her mother sob and her father curse. Marty couldn't move or utter a word.

Much to her relief the judge ordered a break before the coroner testified. She could feel everyone around her moving, but she stayed in her seat, still unmoving and silent. Her mother spoke, but Marty could hardly hear her. She forced herself to snap out of it and she left the courtroom.

Her parents were on a bench near the doorway. Her mother looked withered and shell shocked. Her father—smoldering, chewing on his lower lip, a quirk he had when nervous or angry.

Marty, once again, sat next to them.

"Can I get you something to drink?" she asked them. "Coffee or water or something?"

"Huh?" her father replied.

She repeated herself.

"Yeah, yeah, coffee would be good. Maybe for both of us. I don't even know where to go get it."

"I'll get it. Just stay here."

They both looked at her and nodded. She never knew them to look so helpless.

As she walked to the elevators, she prayed that she wouldn't run into Greg and his family.

When she returned with the coffees, Frank, the prosecutor was on the bench with them. He stood when he saw Marty.

"Hi," he said to her. "Just wanted to see how you're all holding up."

"Barely," she said as she handed the coffee to her parents.

"I know it's rough. There are times when I can't stand hearing this stuff. It's got to be hell for the family."

"Now," he continued. "You don't have to come in after the break. It's, well, it's the coroner. Don't feel that you have to come in for that. You've all heard enough for one day."

"I can't do it," her mother mumbled. "It's harder than I thought it would be. I'm having enough bad dreams. It's too much. Too much. What he did to my boy. My poor boy."

"That's fine," Frank said. "You could stay out here or even go home. You really don't have to stay."

"I'll stay," Marty said. "You can leave if you want to. I don't mind."

Her father nodded.

"I think it's best that we just go on home. She's not holding up too good and to be honest, when I hear what they all been saying, I just want to reach over and kill that little shit with my bare hands. No mercy. Just choke the life out of him."

He looked over at Frank and continued.

"No mercy. You get that rotten little murderer a life sentence. The death penalty would be the best, but you do your job and get him life. You understand?"

"It's not up to me. It's up to the judge and jury."

"You just better do your best to get us some justice."

"I will," Frank replied.

Marty watched them gather their things.

"I'll call you later," she said to them.

"You even know our phone number?" her father said, his anger toward her resurfacing. "It's been a god-damned long time since you even called us."

"You haven't changed it, have you?" she calmly replied.

"It's the same," her mother said. "Call us later. Please just call us. Call me."

"I will."

After they left, Frank looked over at her.

"When the time comes, do you still want to address the court?"

"Yes, now more than ever."

"Any idea what you're going to say?"

"I'm asking for leniency."

"Really," Frank said, "That's a surprise. Leniency. Well, that's not exactly what your father wants."

"I don't care what he wants."

"What brought this on?"

"Mark, Mark brought this on," she said. "Too much misery, more than enough to go around. Maybe something good can come out of this or something less than horrible."

She turned and went back in the courtroom.

Instead of going home after the afternoon testimonies, Marty drove to her parents' home. It was the first time in years that she had been back. It came as no surprise that it hadn't changed much. She could feel her stomach clench as she opened her car door.

Her mother answered, looking renewed and smiling.

"So happy that you came. When you called and said you were coming, well it made me calmer. Calmer and glad."

"Where's dad?"

"In the bedroom watching TV. Bad back. Bothering him a lot today."

"It's late and I can't stay. Can you tell him to come out here? I need to talk to both of you."

"Of course. Sure. Sit down. Get something to drink from the fridge."

"I'm fine," Marty said as she took a seat on the worn sofa. Most of the furniture was there when she left. The only addition was Mark's service photo and the encased American flag on a shelf on the wall.

Her father said nothing as he walked in the room and took his place on the recliner.

Her mother sat next to Marty and folded her hands.

"You didn't miss much," Marty began. "After you left, the coroner spoke and, well, you didn't need to hear it. Some other people testified and then the judge adjourned for the day."

"The reason I came here," she said as she reached for an envelope in her purse, "the reason I'm here is to tell you that Mark left a life insurance policy."

"I told you," her father interrupted, "Didn't I tell you, Judy. What did I tell you?"

"Yes, he left a policy," she continued. "Here."

She handed the envelope to her mother, who began to open it with shaking hands. Her father quickly left the recliner and grabbed it from his wife.

Both stared wide eyed at the Cashier's Check. Marty knew they never saw that amount of money made out to them in their lives.

Her mother—tears forming in her eyes looked away. Her father grinned.

"I knew he wouldn't forget about us. He knew how to be a good son. He did what was right."

Marty took her purse and stood up.

"I was the beneficiary. Not you. I got the money."

"What?" her father yelled. "What the hell you talking about?"

"I was the beneficiary. When I got the check, I turned around and got a cashier's check for the both of you. There's enough there, if you are smart with it, to keep you in decent financial shape for a long while."

They looked at her, confusion written on their faces—both at a loss for words.

"I've got to go. It was a long and miserable day for all of us. If you don't want to return to court, it really is okay. I can call you and tell you what happened."

Her mother spoke up.

"Yeah. If that's all right with you. I'd just as soon not go. It was just too terrible today. And with my high blood pressure, you knew I had high blood pressure, didn't you? Well, it's not good for my high blood pressure and he's got this bad back. The driving is hard. Not like it's close by."

"Like I said, it's fine if you don't go."

"Yeah, it's like your mother said," her father interjected. "But, ah, thanks for bringing the check. That was good of you. We can really use this."

"Yeah, I'm sure you can."

"That's my boy. I'm sure he meant it to come directly to us. He must a made a mistake when he filled out the forms."

She stared down at him.

"Yeah. Right. I'm sure that's it. He was a dummy when it came to filling out forms."

Her sarcasm lost on her father, he replied "Yeah. That's what happened."

With a shake of her head and a curse word she walked out of the home that she once shared with Mark.

My Dead Brother's Journal, continued

Today was brutal. Today was horrible. Hearing the details of the last seconds of Mark's life...I knew what happened, of course. But hearing it in such detail and in such a cold lifeless way from the witness stand, from the cops, the witnesses...I can't shake the words out of my head. The worst part, without a doubt, was the coroner. Suddenly, Mark became a specimen, a clinical object. I wanted to scream at the top of my lungs that he's a person. Not just flesh and bones and ravaged organs. God—it was awful. The logical part of me knows that they're doing their jobs. It's important. I know this. I just hate how he was diminished to mere facts and figures.

Glad Judy and Joe weren't there and don't plan on returning. I don't know what I expected from them. I don't know what they expected from me. I find myself feeling sorry for my mother. What kind of a person, what kind of mother, would she have been, without my father? I think there is a better person in her. And I do believe a mother's grief can be more intense, deeper, more primal. I'll probably keep in touch with her occasionally, but not my greedy, blood sucking father. He was always the worst of the two.

She might understand what I'm going to say to the court. He wouldn't.

I tried not to look at Steven or Greg. Steven looks dazed. Greg looks petrified.

Frank doesn't think the proceedings will take too long. Maybe just a few days more of this. I pray Joe and Judy don't have a change of heart and show up. They'll make what I have to say even harder.

It was the beginning of the following week that Marty was called to speak to the court. The jury didn't take long. Upon hearing the words of the verdict Steven broke down and sobbed, as did his grandmother. Greg sat up straighter and stared ahead. The only movements were the trembling of his hands.

When Frank called on Marty, she took a piece of paper from her purse, dropping it twice before she got to the podium.

She looked over at Steven. This was the first time that Steven looked at her.

He mouthed the words "I'm sorry" with tears streaming down his cheeks.

She glanced over at Greg and nodded.

"Your Honor," she began, "I am the sister of Mark L. Wilder. He was my older brother, my only sibling. We were extremely close. His loss is something that I don't believe I can ever get over. The hole in my heart and in my life is immense.

"Mark was so much more than the person that he was depicted as throughout this hearing. He was so much more than the facts and figures that we heard these last few days. He was smart and funny, generous, stubborn, and loyal. He was a soldier, a very good soldier. And he was the best big brother anyone could have."

Marty paused to take a breath and wipe away the tears. She looked down at the paper in her hands.

"Mark loved kids. He always did. If he could have talked that gun out of Steven's hand he would have. Kids in trouble bothered him. He sometime talked like he wanted to save them all. He coached Little League and spoke at High Schools, always with the hope that maybe there was a troubled kid out there who needed help and he helped. I found, as I was going through his things, that he once spoke at a juvenile detention center.

"I believe that Mark would have liked Steven. I honestly believe that Mark would have listened to Steven in the days and weeks that followed Steven's mother's death. I believe that Mark would have helped Steven work through his grief.

"It's with Mark in mind that I ask for leniency when sentencing Steven. So much tragedy has come out of this incident, I fear for more. Steven is suffering for what he did, as is his family. I've seen enough tragedy. I pray for a sentence that will enable Steven to be young enough when he comes out of this to have a life.

"When this happened, I prayed for the most severe sentence that can be handed down. I've since changed my mind. I think in terms of Mark now. If this had been me who was shot, what would Mark do?

"He would say give this boy a chance. And to Steven," she said as she turned to look at the boy. "He would say, and I say...I forgive you."

Facing the judge, she said. "Thank you for this opportunity to speak."

She left the courtroom.

They met on the same park bench. He had the two coffee containers with him.

He looked better, more alive.

"Eleven years. They gave him eleven years. A chance for parole in seven," he told Marty.

"I'm glad. Eleven years isn't horrible."

"No, it isn't, and initially it will be at a juvenile detention center."

"What's that like?"

"Not as horrible as an adult prison. It's about eighty miles from here. I can see him every week and so can his grandmother and aunt. He'll be able to go to school and continue his education. They give the kids responsibilities. He has to follow strict rules, which I don't think will be a problem for him.

"He'll probably have a roommate. If that's what you call the person you share a cell with. Hopefully a decent one. If he's lucky he may get a single room. But it's still jail time. He'll always have a record. And that cell door is still locked, But it's the best possible outcome. It'll be tough but it could be a lot worse. He understands that."

Marty nodded, not sure of what to say.

"I don't know how to thank you," he continued. "I know what you said made a big difference with the judge. And I know it was good for Steven to hear."

He reached into his jacket pocket.

"He wrote you a letter. I didn't read it. I have no idea what he wrote. But it was important to him that I give it to you personally."

Marty took the envelope.

"Okay, I'll read it later. If that's okay with you."

"Yeah, sure."

"Will you keep me informed, you know, as time goes by?" she asked. "I'll always be wondering about him. He'll always be in the background of my memories of Mark. All part of the same tragedy."

"Yeah, I have your number. I'll stay in touch. You do the same. And again, thank you, from a father."

"You're welcome. I'm glad that this part is over. It's a relief."

"Do you think you'll get a lot of grief from your parents and friends of Mark?" he asked.

"I don't care what my parents think. Unfortunately, they're a minor part of my life. His friends, some will understand. If they really knew Mark, they'll understand."

Greg nodded.

"I feel like a survivor," she said. "I feel like I can now get on with the business of grief. Does that make sense?'

"Yes, it makes a lot of sense. It's something I have to do as well."

"I love this park," she said looking around. "I've been coming here since I moved to Chicago. Even with throngs of tourists, it's a peaceful place to me. Maybe it's the age, the history, the lake. Not sure what."

"Yeah. I get it. There are just places like that."

They finished their drinks in silence, then they walked out of the park together.

The Veteran's Cemetery

Hi. Brought you a new flag and some flowers. And I've become one of those people that talks to headstones in a cemetery. I had a journal—I called it My Dead Brother's Journal. It helped. I stopped writing in it now. Instead, I'll come here and talk to you. I guess justice was done. There are some survivors to my very own tragedy. I'm one of them.

Judy, sorry, I can't bring myself to call her mom. Judy wants me to bring her here. Joe has back issues. He claims that he can't drive this far. I don't know if I'm ready to spend all that time in a car with her. I may give it a shot one day. But only her.

And I'll be doing it for you.

You're with me. Nothing can change that. I know that in one way or another, you'll be taking care of me. You were and are the best big brother ever. Love doesn't end at a gravesite.

I'll try to make you proud of me.

Now I understand why people talk to headstones. For some strange reason, it helps.

I'm going now. But I'll be back. Take it easy or whatever it is that you ghosts do on the other side to kill time.

Second Chances

"I can't believe I let you talk me into this," Donna said to Barbara as they got out of her car. "I must be crazy to go along with this."

"It's something I have to do. Something I've been waiting a lifetime to do." Barbara replied.

"Not a lifetime. Just about fifty years."

"Forty-eight if you want to be precise."

"Barb, he's a world-famous author now."

"Not quite world famous. Just a New York Times best-selling author."

"He's local boy makes good. He's all-over the place. The movie comes out in a month. Why couldn't you have done this before?" Donna said.

"Because I didn't know it was him. I forgot his last name."

"You forgot his last name!" Donna exclaimed.

She repeated. "You forgot his last name. You're unbelievable."

"And he didn't have best sellers until the last five years or so."

"You know he's a lawyer as well," Donna said.

"Yeah. What difference does that make?"

"He's smart. That's what difference that makes. Smart, successful and a millionaire. You're just pissed off that he got away."

"No, I'm not. He's a jerk regardless of how successful and rich he is. He needs to know what happened. He got away with it then. He's got to pay."

"Pay! Barb, he stood you up for the prom forty-eight years ago!" Donna said. "Pay! Pay how? Have your brother beat him up? Your brother who is nearing seventy and probably couldn't care less that you found him. It's not like he murdered someone. It was a lousy prom."

Barbara stopped walking and glared at her friend.

"You have no idea what I went through. Just saving up for the dress and the shoes, getting my hair done. To me it cost a fortune. My folks couldn't afford it, but they gave me what they could. And that's only part of it."

"Alright. Calm down."

"The humiliation was the worse. I had to go back to school on Monday and face everyone. I made up some god-awful story about having food poisoning and how I ended up in the emergency room. I don't think anyone even believed me. It was horrible. It was humiliating in so many ways."

"He didn't call or anything?"

"No. He called a couple days before to ask what color my dress was. I figured it was for the corsage, even though I told him I didn't want one."

"How long did you go out with him?"

"Not long, like three dates. We talked on the phone a lot. Then I asked him, and he seemed fine with the idea. I knew him for a couple of months."

"He went to a different school, right?"

"Yeah, the all-boys Catholic school. I went to an all-girls Catholic school. We met at a dance. He was kind of cute in a nerdy way. Greased back hair and black framed glasses. Thinking back on it, he looked like Buddy Holly. Not my type, but then I really wanted to go to the prom. So, I wasn't being too fussy."

They continued walking toward the venue.

"You never heard from him again?"

"No. My brother said he would try to find him. I don't know what he would have done if he did, but his draft notice came in the next day, and my troubles were ignored.

"God, I cried for days. My father took a picture of me sitting on the sofa waiting. At that point we didn't know he would be a no-show."

"So how did you figure out that this famous author was this jerk from ages ago?" Donna asked.

"Unbelievably, I'm a big fan of his books. When the new one made this big splash there was an interview with him in the Sunday paper. I knew he was from Chicago, but when the article mentioned the high school, I remember thinking—could it be that same jerk—that same Rich that stood me up. Not likely I thought. But I started to Google him and sure enough, there was his high school picture. It's him alright."

"Fine. He was a real asshole," Donna said. "That was a lousy thing to do. But now all these years later, just what do you plan on doing?"

"I don't know."

"You don't know? There's going to be a lot of people there. You'll probably just have to stand in line with everyone else to get your copy signed. And then what?"

"I'll let whoever is in charge know that I'm an old friend, a girlfriend—that's kind of not a lie. I'll wait until it's all over and when he gets ready to leave, I'll go and have a little chat with him."

"You're not armed, are you?"

"Very funny. But I did bring the picture that my dad took of me waiting for him to show up. He needs to know what an awful thing he did, and I want to, no I need to know why. All these years, I always just wondered why he would do something so damn cruel. Then I'll stab him with the hunting knife that I have in my purse."

"Not funny," Donna said. "And you are going to buy me a copy of his book."

"Yes, of course, even though it's only going to enrich him further."

"I'm embarrassed already," Donna said as they walked through the door to the auditorium.

The auditorium was almost at capacity, but they managed to get two seats near the stage. When the moderator introduced him, Donna saw Barb's fingers grip the armrest.

"That's him. That's the bastard," Barb said glaring at the stage.

"Good thing we're in a theatre. Your dramatics fit right in," Donna said. "Maybe they'll give you the stage when this is over."

"Don't mock me. I'm not in the mood."

"You probably can't see this from your angle, but I'm giving you a major eye-roll."

"Hush, I need to hear every word he has to say."

It was during the Q&A that Donna gripped her friend's arm.

"Don't even think about it, Barb. I know what you're thinking. Stop it."

"Just one question—about the book."

"Try it and I'm out the door, without you. Stick to your plan and wait until later."

"Fine." Barb answered, making snake eyes at the stage.

"Everyone's clapping like he's a superstar or something," Barb said when it was over.

"Duh, he is in the literary world."

"His books aren't that great."

'Yes, they are, and you have to admit, he's kind of cute. He's aged well. Lots of hair, no beer belly. Trim and fit."

"Enough, Donna," Barb said loud enough for people to turn around to see who just said that.

"It's true," Donna said with a grin. "He's single, right?"

"How should I know? What kind of question is that?"

"Calm down. I can see that you're getting all atwitter," Donna said as they left the auditorium. "Let's go wait in line, that very, long line that I can see in the distance."

As planned, they loitered around so that they could be at the end of the line.

"Buy me two of his books, while you're at it. We're going to be here a while," Donna said.

"Fine. I'll go get them," Barb said, as she headed over to a group of people who gathered in the corner of the lobby.

His entourage. She thought bitterly.

Donna watched as her friend smiled and addressed the group. They nodded and smiled back.

"What was that all about?" Donna asked when Barb got back, holding the books.

"I told them I was an old friend, an old girlfriend and they said..."

"They said what?"

"Not much. They uttered a few things and just smiled at me."

"Oh geez, this is getting to be a long day."

After letting in a few more people to get in front of them, they were finally in front of him.

"Hi," he said with a smile as he reached out for the books to sign. "Who do I make it out to?"

"Barbara." Unsmiling she repeated her name using her last name, twice.

"Class of 69. St. Mary's High School. Sound familiar?"

"Oh." he said, the smile dropping from his face.

"Oh, yes, Oh." Barbara said.

"Been a long time," he replied.

"Really? Yes, it has been a long time. I want to show you something." She pulled the picture from her purse and handed it to him.

"That's me waiting for you. You, who never showed up."

He looked away from the picture and said nothing.

"For someone who makes his living with words, you don't have much to say."

"What can I say? It was a long time ago. Nice picture. You look nice."

"Dear God, is that all you can come up with? Do you have any idea what I went through, the money I spent, the humiliation I had to endure?" Her voice rising.

Donna looked around praying that they weren't attracting too much attention. So far, the Security Guard hadn't moved.

"Like I said it was a long time ago. I'm sorry."

"Sorry? How about why? How could you not show up for my prom? You had to know how much it meant to me."

"I was a stupid, selfish teenager. What can I say?"

"What can you say? I'll tell you what you can say. You can tell me why. You say where you were and why you didn't even have the decency to call and apologize. That's what you can say."

"Christ, Barb. You want to cool it with the dramatics," Donna interjected. "This is getting embarrassing."

"You want to know why? Well, here it is," he answered. "I got together with my friends earlier that afternoon and we got stoned. We sat around and got stoned. Before you knew it, it was time to pick you up and all we could do was laugh our asses off about a prom and pass another joint."

"That's it? You got stoned," she said. "Damn, I was really hoping for something good, like a car accident that left you without a memory. Or a death in the family. But that's it. You got stoned. It never occurred to you to call and apologize?"

"And face what I did. No way. Too much of a coward. Easier to ignore the whole situation."

"Your parents. Didn't they notice that you weren't going to the prom that you must have rented a tux for?"

"My ma was at work and my old man was getting hammered with his buddies at the bar on the corner. They really didn't give a shit if I went to a prom or not."

Barb stood there gaping at him with a loss for words.

"Pretty anticlimactic, if you ask me," Donna piped in.

"This is my friend Donna," Barb finally said.

"Hi," she said, reaching her hand out to shake his. "Good times, huh? Nothing like reminiscing about the good old days."

She handed him a book and told him to make it out to "Donna, Barb's friend".

They watched him sign it.

"So now what?" Donna asked.

Rich looked up at Barb.

"I am sorry," he said. "Just a stupid teenage episode. I can't change what happened."

Barb nodded.

"You look good," he said to her. "You really haven't changed much."

"Either have you," she said softly.

"Are you married? Working. What?" he asked.

"Divorced ages ago. One kid. I worked at an insurance company for years. Just retired. Nothing as glamorous as your life," she replied. "What about you, apart from the obvious?"

"Married three times, divorced three times. Two kids, girls."

"Guess you never could stop screwing things up," Donna said.

"Donna!" Barb said.

"What?"

"She's right," Rich said. "I messed up a lot. Maybe that's why I write books. My character can fix things and the bad guys always get what's coming to them."

"Anyway," he continued. "Let me make it up to you."

"It better be good. She's carrying a major grudge," Donna said.

"I'll be in town for a couple of days. Let's go out for dinner."

"Um, okay, I guess."

"Today's not good. I have a radio interview after this. How about tomorrow?"

"Um, okay."

Donna reached over, grabbed Barb's arm and pulled her away from the table.

"You'll have to excuse us for a moment," she said to Rich.

"That's all you have to say, Barb,"

"What do you want me to say?"

"The whole time coming over here, you bitched up a storm, now you're like 'okay'. Whatever you say Rich. I think you're even fluttering your eyelashes."

"Well, he did say he was sorry, and it was a long time ago."

"And you're considering going out to dinner with him."

"Sure, why not?"

"Because he's been married three times."

"So. A lot of people get married three times. Not a crime."

"And I don't like him."

"What? You've just met him and exchanged a few words, and you don't like him."

"I'm a good judge of character and I don't trust him or like him. He probably still has some of that stupid, teenager running through his system. Some people just get older, not better."

"Really Donna, you're not making much sense."

Barb left her friend standing there and went back to the table.

"I would love to have dinner with you tomorrow," she told him.

"Great," he said with a smile. "Let bygones be bygones, as they say."

"All right," she smiled right back.

"Forgive and forget," he said.

"Sure, forgive and forget."

They shook hands.

He named a restaurant not far from where they were, which meant driving back to the city from the suburbs a second day in a row.

"Not a problem. I'll be there," Barb said with a huge smile.

"7:00?"

"7:00."

"I really have to go. But I'll see you tomorrow," he said.

"Great, see you tomorrow."

The drive back home was in silence for most of the ride.

"So, you're not going to speak to me because I agreed to have dinner with him," Barb started. "A simple dinner."

"It won't be a simple dinner. I know you. You'll get a new dress and get your hair done and drive back down here, even though you hate driving down here, which is why I'm driving. He's probably staying at a nice hotel in walking distance from the restaurant."

"I would regret not doing this," Barb replied. "We're not kids anymore. I don't see what's wrong with meeting him for dinner."

"I'll keep my mouth shut and withhold judgement until the morning after when you call me to let me know what happened. You embarrassed him today. Don't think you didn't."

"You're turning this into a big deal and it's not. It's dinner with someone from my past, who will be leaving town in a couple of days. And I'll call you and let you know how it went. I'm sure it'll be a pleasant evening."

"Be sure to ask him if he still smokes dope. Or is he alcohol dependent now."

"For Pete's sake, Donna. Can we just drop it?"

When they pulled up in front of Barbara's condo, Donna said, "Barb, I do hope it goes well. I really do. Just don't expect too much. Hope you have a nice time."

"I will. Thanks, and thanks for driving and being there for me."

"What are friends for?"

"For times like this. Thanks again and I'll talk to you the morning after."

"Yeah, well, I hope you call me from home, not a hotel room."

"God, Donna, how stupid do you think I am?"

"Yeah, well, I guess we just have to wait and see what happens."

Barb did get a new dress and shoes but couldn't get in to have her hair done.

She sighed when she looked in the mirror and saw the woman that the young teenager had become.

It's called getting older, she thought as she walked to her car. *Can't stop it. Just have to make the best of it. He's older too.*

An hour and a half after the time set for dinner, Barbara was driving home, fighting back tears of rage. She tried to make excuses for him. He didn't have her number. But he could have called the restaurant and they could have told her he wasn't coming and maybe why.

Instead, she sat on the seat near the doorway of the restaurant...waiting.

The worst part was going to be telling her best friend that she was right.

 Voyagers

I can still remember, despite all the intervening years, the first time that I saw him. He was shy, or maybe just afraid. We were a raucous group of kids—loud, covered in play-time dirt and sweat, unconcerned and unaffected by the lives billowing around us. And it was the beginning of summer.

He was new to this neighborhood. I'm sure he had no idea how harmless we were. If you were a kid and could throw a ball or run with any speed, you would be included in our games. It didn't matter if you were a boy or a girl. When it came to whatever game we were playing, we were a very democratic group.

But he stood by a park bench and just watched. It bothered me, but apparently no one else. So, I approached him.

I remember how his eyes widened as I got near to him.

"Hi," I said. "I'm Annie. My name is really Anna Marie, but everyone just calls me Annie. What's your name?"

He looked me up and down. I saw his lips move, but he said nothing. I prevailed.

"You live around here? Never saw you before."

"Karol." He muttered.

"Huh?"

This he said not looking at me but past me.

"Karol." He repeated. I picked up on the accent.

"Carol? That's a girl's name."

He didn't reply and looked around. He seemed determined not to make eye contact with me.

I was not to be deterred.

"I think I'll just call you Carl and tell the other kids your name is Carl."

He shrugged.

"You live around here or just like, you know, visiting someone?"

"Live here, now. That house." He pointed to one of the two flats across from the park.

"Where do go to school?" This was an important question. Since the school you went to was determined by your nationality. The Polish school, the Lithuanian school, the Slovak school. It was simply an important question.

Once again, he shrugged.

I was used to the adults in the neighborhood having foreign accents, but not the kids. I was intrigued.

"Where you from?"

"Krakow, Poland," he answered. He said it in such a pained manner that I wasn't sure what to say next.

"Poland. Lots a people here from Poland. My grandmother is from Poland. That's my father's mother. My mother's mother is from Lithuania. You ever heard of Lithuania?"

He nodded yes, looking down at the pavement.

"You'll probably go to Sacred Heart. A lot of Polish kids go there. You'll like it."

There was no response this time.

"You want to come over and meet the other kids. We're playing Simon Says."

He finally looked at me, but I could see how puzzled he was.

"Come on," I persisted. "It's okay."

He shook his head no.

"Ya sure? It's fun."

Again, he shook his head no and began to walk away, slowly with his hands in his pockets.

"Well, we'll probably be here tomorrow," I called after him. "Sometimes, we play in the alley and sometimes on the street. But you can always play with us."

He continued walking.

"Bye, Carl. See ya."

He didn't look back. I kept on watching, until I saw what house he went into.

The other kids asked about him when I rejoined them.

I told them what little I knew.

"He sure is clean. I bet he didn't want to get his clothes dirty. They looked brand new," Dennis said.

"Kinda weird the way he just watched us," Ethel piped in.

"He has broken English. He's from Poland," I told them.

"Never met a kid from Poland. I just thought old people came from Poland," Pete said.

"Well, we have to be nice to him," I ordered. "He's probably scared. I bet he can't hardly speak a lot of English."

This began my fixation on my new friend Carl.

I began walking down that street and going to the park more often with the hope of seeing him again.

It wasn't long before I did.

Once again, it was in the park. Once again, he stood in the distance and watched us. I stopped playing and ran over to him.

"Hi, Carl. How ya doin'?" I asked.

He gave me a small smile.

"It's okay if you don't know a lot of English. We're used to that around here. A lot of the old people don't talk in English and us kids understand them just fine."

"So," I continued. "How'd ya like it here?"

He shrugged. The shrugs were getting annoying.

"We like it here okay. Lots to do in the summer. Did you know that there's a swimming pool on the other side of the park? It's for everyone."

"Yes, I know."

Finally!

"You got any brothers or sisters?"

"No."

"Hmm, just you and you mom and dad?"

"No," he said with a frown.

"No?"

"My uncle and my auntie, only."

"Oh." I didn't know what to say next.

I didn't want him to wander off again, so I carried on.

"Ya sure you don't want to meet the other kids. They're real nice."

"No, tank you. No."

"Okay. I live on the next block. The two-story made of brick next to the grocery store. We're on the first floor. If you ever want to play or anything, just come and get me. Okay?" I said with my biggest smile.

He gave me a small smile back and said "Okay."

It was a small victory for me. I sensed that he was sad, very sad, so I felt it best to leave him alone.

Two days later, I looked out my front window and across the street stood Carl. I bolted from the house and ran over to him.

"Hi, Carl."

"Hello."

"How's it going?"

"Goot."

Not knowing what to say next, I asked him if he wanted to go for a walk. He nodded yes.

I gave him a tour of my block and the adjoining blocks. I pointed out the highlights—the tavern where most of the men went to but was also the place where they had weddings and other kinds of parties. Then there was the church rectory and another grocery store that had a great selection of candy. I filled him in on the current occupants of the houses that I knew.

He listened patiently and said little, at times he looked perplexed.

"Vere is church?" he asked.

I took him over to the next block and I showed him one of many churches in our neighborhood.

"This is the Polish one. You'll probably go to their school."

Silently, he went up the stairs to the church, opened the door and went in. I followed.

He dabbed his finger in the holy water font, crossed himself, genuflected and went into a pew. I did the same.

He knelt and began to pray. I saw that he was crying.

I left him alone and wandered the small church. It was empty except for an old lady cleaning one of the statues.

When I looked over, he had stood up and was wiping away his tears. We left the church in silence.

On the way home, neither of us spoke.

When we got to my house, he finally did.

"Tank you. I pray for mama and papa. I go home now. Tank you. All right if I come again?"

"Yeah, sure. Anytime. I'll show you some other stuff like the movie theater. Maybe you can go with us kids and see a movie"

"Yes, that vould be good."

"Yeah, it would. Okay. And like my father would say—Don't be a stranger," I said with my biggest smile and went inside. I watched him from the front window as he walked down the street.

I decided to confront the adults for information. I started with my mother. I watched as she ironed our father's shirt. I was always mesmerized watching the wrinkles flatten out so quickly.

"Do you know anything about the Polish kid on the next block. He lives in a flat across from the park with his uncle and aunt. Has no brothers or sisters. It's just him."

"No. Haven't heard anything about that. How do you know him?" she answered.

"He came to the park when we were playing. I was talking to him. He doesn't know too much English but said he was from Poland. He seems nice."

"Is that who you were just walking around with?"

"Yeah. His name is Carl. We went inside the church and when he was praying, he started to cry. Said he was crying for his mama and papa. I wish I knew what he was talking about. He's so sad."

"Hmm. A lot of people are coming from the old country. The Russians are making it real hard for them. Things are a lot better here."

"But without his mother and father?" I asked, bewildered.

"I really don't know anything about it, but you know who will."

I was hoping she wouldn't suggest this, but she did.

"Babka Mary."

I let out a groan.

"She knows everyone and everything if it has to do with the Poles. I'm sure she knows all about it."

"I know. I know. But it's Babka Mary."

"Don't be disrespectful. She's still your grandmother."

And my personal embarrassment. The kids were not only afraid of her, but they also made fun of her. And she was my grandmother. She never hesitated to scream at you or even hit you if you did anything to annoy her. The adults were wary of her because of her strange ways. She would chastise them as much as she would the children. Babka Mary never held back.

I had heard conversations about her. Adults sometimes thought that kids were deaf when they were around. Someone once said that she was tetched in the head. Someone else said that it was because three of her children died when they were young, under five years old, and she never got over it. And then her husband died in a grizzly accident at the nearby coal yard. She was left to raise the remaining seven children on her own. There was no money and mouths to feed. That's when she became tetched. She got a part-time job as a janitress but that paid little. They were always on the brink of starvation. One old woman said that she was a nice young girl when they came over from Poland, very pretty, but all the death and the poverty gave her a nervous breakdown and made her this way.

By "this way" meant obsessively sweeping the street in front of her two flat dressed in all manner of strange clothing—men's shoes, worn babushkas wrapped tightly around the top of her head, raggedy old dresses, gloves—even in the summer.

My mother said that she had money for new clothes but wouldn't spend it. She went through the garbage cans in the alleys looking for thrown out clothing. Even when people, including my parents gave her something new to wear, she would only wear it to church. Most of the new things were never worn and packed away in a trunk in her closet. My parents gave up giving her new clothes.

By spending so much time outdoors sweeping the sidewalks and when not fighting with a neighbor, she would get all the local news. There was no hesitation when it came to asking questions and snooping into other lives.

Yes, Babka Mary would know.

It was with my dogged need to know about Carl that I found myself in front of the door to Babka's flat, armed with pastries from the Polish Bakery. I said a silent prayer that the visit would be a short one.

"Hello Babka!" I said with my biggest smile.

She looked down at me without displaying any emotion.

"It's me. Annie."

She opened the door wider and went back to her seat in front of the television. When not sweeping the front sidewalk and chastising the immediate population, Babka Mary's other obsession was the television soap operas. No matter what we said to the contrary, she believed these shows were real. The people real, their stories real.

This was the other reason that she was said to be tetched in the head.

I timed my visit after the last of her favorite soap operas was over, otherwise she wouldn't answer the door. Even though the shows were over, she sat in front of the now quiet television pondering today's events.

I stood in front of her and gave her the pastries.

"How are you Babka?"

She nodded and stuffed a pastry in her mouth.

Babka was never an affectionate grandmother. She was unlike my other grandmother, Polly who always smothered us with hugs and wet kisses. Babka looked at us as incidentals. We were something that happened, not worthy of too much attention.

How did my father ever survive having her as a mother, I often wondered?

I got right to the point.

"Babka, do you know the little Polish boy that lives with his uncle and aunt across the street from the park? I met him and he doesn't know too much English and me and my friends want to be his friend, but we don't know anything about him."

She wiped her mouth with the hem of her dress and nodded.

"Sit," she ordered.

I sat.

"His name Karol Wojewski, from Krakow. His mother and father in jail. They send him here to live with his mother's sister."

I was stunned. In jail!

"Why are they in jail, Babka?"

69

"Russians no like them. They think they so smart and never stop talking against the Russians, so they put them in jail."

"How did Carl get here?"

She shrugged.

"How they all get here? Somebody hide boy, get him on boat and send him here."

"Will they get out of jail and come here?"

She shrugged again.

"Maybe yes, maybe no. Lots die in Russian jails. Not good to be in Russian jail. Should not talk against Russians. They mean, real mean."

I looked around not sure what to say or ask next.

"That's terrible. Poor Carl."

She stuffed another pastry in her mouth.

"You being good girl?" she asked.

"Yes, Babka, I'm being good," I replied distractedly.

"Your brother and sister?"

"Yes, we're all being good."

"Go to church?"

"Yes, we're all going to church. Are you okay?"

"I fine, but that Robert no good to his wife. I think he leave his wife for kurva girlfriend."

I knew she was referring to a soap opera character and decided to end the visit.

I leaned over and kissed her on the powdered sugar cheek.

"I'm going now, Babka."

"Hmm. You be good girl. Be nice to Karol. He sad and miss his mama and papa and Krakow. He miss Poland. Like me."

"I will, Babka. I will."

Even though it was drizzling, I walked back home slowly.

Prison. A Russian jail. I didn't even know what to imagine. I felt so sorry for Carl. He was about my age and had been through so much.

I stood under a tree when the rain got heavier, not really caring that I was getting wet.

How should I talk to him the next I saw him? Should I tell him I know his story? Or should I wait until he told me.

My mother answered that question when I got home as she towel-dried my hair.

"You mind your own business and don't say a thing to him about what Babka told you. If he wants you to know, he'll tell you. Maybe not now, but sometime in the future. It must be a terrible thing to live with. Poor boy. So just treat him like a normal kid. Help him with his English and just be nice. That's probably all he needs right now."

I followed her advice. I never let him know what I knew. Gradually, he began to talk to the other kids and by the end of the summer, he was playing our weird style of baseball. The first time I heard him laugh, I wanted to cry.

He went to see a few movies with us and seemed to understand what was happening. His English improved. He was assimilating.

I never shared any of my knowledge with the other kids. It was my secret. Well, it was Carl's and my secret.

We still took walks, sometimes little was said. I was alright with that. It seemed like he was too.

Once school started, we saw less of each other since we went to different schools. We still took our walks, usually to one of the parks and usually on weekends—until the snows and frigid temperatures came. When the weather improved, we reconnected.

A year flew by and once again, our lives settled around games and movies and television. Carl's English had greatly improved. His grades didn't suffer because of his English. He was gradually losing his thick accent. I was told that he was considered the smartest kid in his class.

I was far from that.

It was on a hot summer morning when our front door opened and in walked Babka Mary. This was a rare event, and I knew something monumental had to happen to bring her here.

She headed directly for me and grabbed me by the shoulders.

"His mama and papa. They dead. Die in Russian prison."

Words failed me. I stared at her and nodded.

"He know. They tell him. He know."

I nodded again.

With that she turned around and left the flat, ignoring my mother and my brother and sister.

"What the heck was that all about?" my brother asked.

My mother looked at me.

"Carl?" she asked.

"Yeah. What should I do, Mom?"

"Go to him. He needs a friend now. Tell him that you know and just be there. Take him to church if he hasn't been there yet."

"Yeah, okay," I said, once again ready to follow my mother's advice.

When I got to his flat, I could hear the weeping through the apartment door. It came from his aunt, his mother's sister. I knocked.

The door was opened by a parish priest. Carl was sitting in an armchair by the window, his arms wrapped around his knees. His eyes a deep red from crying. He looked small and bruised.

The adults were huddled around the dining room table speaking softly. No one said anything to me.

I walked over to Carl.

"You want to go for a walk?" I asked.

He nodded yes and said something in Polish to his aunt. She wiped at her eyes and said something in return.

She smiled weakly at me. I knew I should say something to her but all that came out was "I'm sorry."

"Dziękuję," she replied.

We walked over to the park and sat on a bench.

"How did you find out?" he asked.

"How else? Babka Mary."

He let out a small sound and shook his head.

"I knew for a long time about them," I admitted.

"What?"

"Babka told me last summer. I never told you that I knew."

"I think that was good. I did not want to talk about it."

"You can talk about it now. If you want, I mean."

He said nothing for a while.

"They were called Dysydentów. I think the English is dissidents," he began. "They hate the Soviets. They talk against them. My father was a teacher. But he, too, ran a small newspaper and wrote against them. My mother helped. They should have not done this. They knew what could happen. But they wanted free Poland. We suffered so much during the war.

"The night the Soviet police were coming, someone told them. They put me in a bundle and in the back seat of a car with strangers, on the floor. Mama was crying. So was papa. I so scared. They telling me it would all be fine. I should do what these people tell me to do.

"I cried even when my papa said to be a big boy. I slept much and cried when I was not sleeping. Then I was in Amsterdam with more strangers. After a long time there, a couple of months I think, I go to London. Then I was on a boat coming to America, farther and farther away from mama and papa.

"I did what everyone told me to do. Someone always saying that mama and papa would find me and come to me some day. I believed them.

"Then I was here with auntie and uncle. And here I stay. No mama and no papa."

At that he broke down in sobs. I patted his back, not sure what to do.

When he stopped crying, he said, "The Russians said they were traitors and shot them." He looked over at me.

Another stunning detail for me to absorb. I wanted to cry but didn't for his sake.

"Not traitors. Patriots. Want a better Poland. You know, a free Poland."

I nodded and said yes. I know, I told him. I understand, I told him. But I really didn't. I could never understand that kind of bravery or fear. Or sacrifice.

Walking back to the flat, he held my hand. I let him.

Babka Mary in her best dress, my mother, father and I went to the mass that was being said for the souls of Karel's parents. Coming back from communion I glanced over and caught Carl's eye. He gave me a small smile. I gave him a small smile back.

Time and changes came rapidly.

Carl and I maintained our friendship throughout high school. Most of our childhood friends drifted off in several directions. But with Carl, it was still slow walks on summer evenings, now supplemented by bus rides downtown and lake front walks and movies.

I had my girlfriends, but I could never talk to them the way I could with Carl.

He had the maturity I lacked. He never failed to make the honor role. I never failed to barely get passing grades. He was disciplined. I wasn't. He feared and obeyed anyone in authority. I questioned and railed against them. I was the poster child for the rebellious sixties. He was the conservative on the sidelines.

Simply put—he was my best friend.

It was near to our approaching graduations, during one of our lake front walks after a downtown movie, when we talked and laughed about our proms, which happened to have been on the same day. He went with someone that I approved of. I went with someone that he thought would be a bad influence on me. Nothing came of either relationship.

It was abrupt when he said it. He said that his uncle and aunt bought a house and were moving to one of the suburbs. I suddenly remembered the word—gobsmacked. I must have heard it in a British movie. That was how I felt—gobsmacked. I stopped walking. I knew that he was going to college in September, on a full scholarship, of course. He would be only an hour and a half away. I would see him on holidays and some weekends. But this was different.

I could suddenly see the future. Carl getting his degrees, becoming a success, getting married and having children, really moving away, maybe back to Poland.

My breath seemed to catch in my throat.

I didn't reply for a while. I finally looked over at him and said in an almost panicked voice.

"This is life, isn't it, Carl? People come and go in each other's lives. They get pulled apart and have no choice in the matter. People move away from each other and become names in an old address book and send Christmas cards to each other."

"Yes. I know that can happen, Annie. But it doesn't have to be that way. Not all relationships are so fragile. They survive the changes. I'm going to college and my uncle and aunt are moving to the suburbs. Life will put you on a course also. Did you really think we both could stay in one place forever?"

"I know. I know. I guess I'm just feeling, I don't know, scared. So much is happening around us. Sometimes I just want to be a little kid again and play in the park."

"I understand what you are saying, but at the same time, I want to grow up and manage my own life," he replied.

"Of course, you do. Do you want to manage mine too? I don't know if I'll be any good at it."

He laughed.

"Annie, you will do great. You will be fine. It's the world that may not be ready for you."

It was two days later when my father went to visit Babka Mary and bring her lunch that he found her dead. The television was blaring the latest soap opera atrocity.

"Must have been that Erica on All My Children that did her in," he told us that evening. We had a good laugh, and the line was repeated several times at the wake.

Carl came with his aunt and uncle, as did most of the neighborhood.

He stood next to me at the casket and we stared together at her waxen body.

"Nice dress," he said.

"Her favorite dress that she never wore," I replied.

"No babushka?" he asked.

"My parents stopped me."

"She looks so normal."

I nodded and tears bubbled up.

He looked over and frowned.

"You want to get out of here and go for a walk?"

I nodded yes and we quickly walked by the mass of people that had accumulated in the room.

"I'm not sure why I'm crying. She was a lousy grandmother. Most of the time I was embarrassed by her."

"She had a good heart."

"Yeah, she did. I guess," I replied, remembering the day that she told me about Carl's parent's death. "I think I'm sad because life treated her so awful. So awful that she went nuts. I mean three of her kids died when they were little and then her husband. And they were so poor. She was pretty and normal when she got here from Poland. I've seen the pictures. But she died a mad woman, mocked and disliked, even by her family."

"You put it that way and I may start to cry."

He paused, then said, "I never told you this, but she came to see me when she heard about my parents. She didn't want to see my aunt or uncle. Just me."

"Really? What happened?"

"She talked about Poland. About the family she left behind, about the farms and the landscape, the food, the music. Everything and anything that she could remember. It went on well into the night."

"Definitely sounds like something she would do."

"It felt so good to hear her stories. I needed to hear them. I slept well that night. No tears. Just, I don't know, a feeling of warmth. I never forgot that. She never spoke to me again. An occasional smile, like we had a secret, but never another conversation. I guess I loved her for that."

We walked in silence for another couple of blocks, deep in thought.

"After my dad and my uncles made the funeral arrangements," I said, "he and mom called us three kids together and told us that we'll be selling our house and getting a place in Oak Lawn."

Carl looked over and said nothing.

"Life goes on," I said.

"Life goes on," he repeated.

A few weeks later, we both graduated from high school. His, a week later than mine. Mine overshadowed by the assassination of Robert Kennedy. My graduation party turned out to be a somber affair. But in keeping with traditions, there were plenty of cousins, uncles and aunts to congratulate me and pepper me with questions that I didn't have answers to.

I went to Carl's graduation ceremony and his party with my parents. There were few relatives, but enough friends and neighbors to make up the difference.

"So hotshot, did you win enough honors and awards?" I asked flippantly, knowing that he graduated at the top of his class.

"Yes," he smiled. "I believe I did. And did you win any honors or awards?"

"Hell, no. I'm lucky I graduated."

We both laughed.

"When this thins out you want to sit outside on the back porch?" he asked, his accent subtle but still there.

"Sure. In the meantime, I'll go get my share of pierogis and kielbasa."

It wasn't quite dark out yet when I joined him on the back porch. The lightning bugs were popping out, and the air had the scent of freshly mowed grass. A few of our friends left to go to another party where there would be enough alcohol to keep them busy. We both declined to join them.

At first, we spoke in generalities and gossip. Then settled back to our familiar silences.

I spoke first.

"You will be happy to know that I've made a decision."

"A decision from you is definitely something to celebrate."

"Do you want to know what it is?"

"Of course."

"I am going to be a stewardess—an airline stewardess. I've been checking into it and it's what I want to do. I want to fly to cities all over this country and maybe eventually all over the world. I know I can't sit in an office all day or work in a department store. I want to let loose and see the world and meet interesting people, just live."

Carl grinned and nodded.

"Yes, I can see you as an airline stewardess. You are so much smarter than you think you are, and you are without a doubt, pretty enough."

"Wow Carl, a complement on my looks. That's a first." This coming from this handsome blond-haired young man.

"I do notice these things, Annie," he said with a smile. "And what is the first step to becoming an airline stewardess."

"Well, my mother and I talked about it. I have a cousin who works for United. It was actually his idea. He knows where to apply and if I have questions, he can ask the stewardesses that he works with. But first things first."

"I did get that job at the phone company that I applied for," I continued. "Sounds boring. Anyway, I'll stay there for a year before going to the airlines. I'll need some work experience. And I'm going to take night classes at the community college. That'll look good too. Maybe study geography."

"Have you ever been on a plane?"

"Yes, remember last year when my aunt took me to California with her? I loved it. Wasn't nervous or scared. I will do this Carl. I really want to do this. Maybe someday, you'll get a postcard from me from Paris. Wouldn't that be great?"

"Yes, Annie. That would be great. I'm happy to hear this. I'm happy that you are making plans. You would not be happy, like you said, sitting in an office. You have so much life in you, so much energy."

"And you, Carl. What have you decided on?"

"I will be an engineer."

"Like on a choo-choo train?"

"Yes, of course, like on a choo-choo train."

We laughed and made follow-up remarks until it was hard to stop our giggling.

After a while he took a breath and said. "Aerospace engineer. An aerospace engineer. Annie, we are sending men to the moon. This is such an exciting time. Maybe I can be a small part of that. Who knows what the future can bring? Yes, aerospace engineer. It will take a long time and a lot of study and work, but, like you, I am determined to do this."

"Wow, your dreams are much bigger than mine."

"But just as important."

"I know you can do it, Carl."

"And I know you can do it, Annie."

"Strange that we're talking about the future, isn't it?"

"Are you still frightened of it?" he asked.

"No. I think I just get frightened of never seeing you again."

"That will not happen. We must not let that happen."

We listened to the night sounds around us. I could hear the street traffic and the clatter of dishes coming from the kitchen.

"We are going in different directions, but we must stay together," he said.

"I'll be jetting off to foreign lands and you'll be doing whatever it is that aerospace engineers do. We are so different, Carl, you and me. I can't sit still. I'm restless. I want to see everything and do everything. You are calm and steady. I move fast without thinking. You study and analyze before moving."

"We're so incompatible." I added.

"Does that mean we should not get married?"

My heart stopped in my chest. I knew he wasn't making a joke. I looked him in the eye.

"It wouldn't work," I said in a shaky voice. "We would hold each other back. We could end up hurting each other. And I can't bear the thought of that."

"Me either," he said.

"I'm not even sure of what we would talk about," I said.

"I would worry about plane crashes," he said.

"Our schedules would be crazy," I said.

"I would have so much studying to do," he said.

"You would be studying in some old library and I'd be somewhere on a beach in California," I said.

"I would worry that you would run off with a pilot or a celebrity," he said.

"I would worry about the cute, smart girls on campus," I said.

"You are right, Annie. It's true. We would damage each other," he said.

"We could crush each other's dreams," I said.

"We would fight," he said.

"We never fight. That would be awful," I said.

I found it hard to say another word. He didn't.

"Annie," he said softly, "Maybe this is the Polish romantic coming out in me, but you are, and always will be my great love. The love of my life. You have been since the day I met you as a scared young kid. No matter where our lives take us, I will never stop loving you."

I felt tears stream down my cheeks. I reached for his hand.

"And I will never stop loving you, Carl. I can't imagine a life that you are not a part of. No one will ever come between us. We may not marry each other, but we can and always will love each other."

For the first time, he kissed me—a warm, lingering kiss. I gently kissed him back. He wiped away my tears.

Then I walked out into that warm, summer evening.

In the next few months, we saw each other sporadically. He helped us move to the new house in Oak Lawn. There were no more conversations like the one we had on graduation night, but there were the looks, the warm smiles, and the walks. We somehow found time to take walks and talk about all that was happening around us.

Life went on as planned. I worked for a year at the phone company, then applied at United Airlines and was hired. My first call was to Carl to tell him the news. I sent him a postcard from the first city that I landed in.

Carl studied, worked hard and made excellent grades.

And the years went by.

I started on International flights and sent him a postcard from Paris, knowing I would be home before the postcard.

I had my own apartment near the airport.

Carl went on to get his Masters. Even before he completed his classes, he was recruited by a major aeronautics company.

He found time to date. As did I. We shared some of our experiences.

He called me on a Saturday night.

"Remember Rose, the girl I've been seeing?"

"Yes, of course. The history major. She's the one that wants to teach history, right? Sounds like you really like her."

"I do, Annie. I do. I'm going to ask her to marry me."

Again, I felt gobsmacked and couldn't speak.

"Annie, are you there?"

"Uh, yeah. I'm just kind of shocked. I didn't know how serious it was. Wow," I said, my heart was racing.

"We get along so beautifully. She's brilliant and sweet. We have a lot in common."

"Yeah, I figured that out when you started to bring her up."

"I want you to be happy for me."

"I am," I said, meaning it. "I am happy for you Carl. I really am. I'm dying to meet her. We have to figure something out. Let's get together."

"Yes, I really want you to meet her. You will like her. I know you will."

And I did.

I was in Europe the day of their wedding. Carl said that he understood. It was a small wedding at the University's chapel. A few family and friends followed by a luncheon.

I called him when I was back in the states.

"No pierogis, and kielbasa and polka band?" I asked.

"No, a very subdued event. Rose wanted it that way. And it was fine with me. Uncle and Auntie came. They like her."

"She is really sweet, and I know you'll be happy."

"Thank you, Annie and thank you for the lovely gift. It was very thoughtful."

I sent them a hand carved Polish crystal vase.

"And very Polish I might add."

"Yes, very Polish."

"I'll see you soon?"

"Yes, Rose wants you to come to dinner. She is a really good cook."

"I'd like that, Carl. I really would."

"I'll call you soon."

"Yes, please do."

I hung up, opened a bottle of wine and had a good cry.

The years became decades. There were friend's weddings, baby announcements, family funerals—my father first, then Carl's aunt, followed two years later by his uncle. We stood side by side at these events.

I'd flown thousands of miles and saw countries and cities that some people just dream about.

Carl landed an impressive job with a huge aeronautics company. Rose gave birth to two boys in the first four years of marriage. They bought a two-story colonial in an affluent suburb.

We still saw each other, usually over dinners or lunches. I became a surrogate aunt for the boys, bringing them gifts from all parts of the world. Rose was always nice, but withdrawn and quiet when I was around. She never displayed any jealousy, but I think she knew that there was a world that Carl and I were in that she had no part of.

It was after twenty years of flying that I stopped. The nineties were upon us. We were flight attendants now. And I was tired. So much had changed in the airline industry and the world. I had seen all there was to see. Except for Poland. Once the Soviet Union collapsed, I wanted to see Poland, but it had to be with Carl.

I had a ten-year relationship with someone from the airline that ended with mutual consent. The topic of marriage and having children began to happen more often. I would change the subject or make feeble excuses as to why I couldn't commit. It was simply a threshold that I couldn't cross. A commitment that I couldn't make—not with him. I stayed away so that he could pack. Then he was gone.

It was a warm summer day when I called Carl to let him know that I had quit my job. He didn't say much.

"What now, Annie?"

"I don't know. I need some time off to think."

"Can we meet somewhere, maybe Lincoln Park, like we used to?"

I paused.

"Yes. I would like that. A bench in Lincoln Park, like we used to."

We settled on the day and time.

I saw him in the distance, sitting on the bench, a bit older, a bit grayer. He looked pensive, deep in thought. My heart skipped a beat.

He stood up and hugged me.

I started on preliminary small talk. He held up his hand and nodded no.

"What's wrong?" I asked

He breathed a loud sigh.

"Both boys now have graduated from high school. Philip will follow his brother at the University in September."

"Yes, I know."

"It was the time that Rose and I waited for, no, not waited, agreed to."

I said nothing.

"Rose and I are getting a divorce."

"What?"

"It was not a good marriage. Not for many years. We didn't fight. No arguing. We just stopped talking. We stopped doing things together. We lived together, just lived together in different worlds. We waited for the boys to get old enough so as not to traumatize them with separate homes."

"How did the boys take the news?" I asked, trying to mask the quiver in my voice.

"They seem fine with it," he said. "Children sense things. They said that they knew things were not right with us. They both said that they want us to be happy. They will be off to college in a couple of months, unscathed, ready to take on life without us."

"I don't know what to say. I'm sorry. I really am. I thought you were happy."

"I tried to be and failed."

"Where are you living?"

"Still at the house. In a couple of weeks, I move to a small studio apartment near the office. She will get the house, and some money. I will pay for the boys' college. They have a college fund, but what the fund doesn't cover I will."

We watched the sail boats on the lake.

He finally said, "So, what are you going to do for employment, or do you have wealth I don't know about."

"Yeah, tons of wealth," I replied. "I know a travel agent here in downtown. She offered me a job. I'm going to take it."

"You will stay in one place every day?" he smiled.

"Yes, and I think I will be glad to. It might be fun to tell people about the places I've been and what they should and shouldn't do when they travel. I'm looking forward to it," I said. "And you, how's your position?"

"It's becoming a young man's job. I am an administrator now. A boss. And like you, I tell my staff what I know and what they should and shouldn't do. I'm adjusting."

Once again, a silence, a comfortable silence.

He spoke first.

"Annie."

"Yes, Carl."

"Annie, I think we can get married now."

"Yes, Carl, my love, we can get married now."

And we did.

We went to Poland for our honeymoon. A much more romantic place than people think. We found his childhood home. I held his hand as the memories swept by. I held him when he wept.

It bothered him that there was no grave to visit. We did find other graves, other names, other relatives.

We bought a small house on a big lot in an older, heavily wooded, northern town. I eventually quit the downtown job and took one closer to our home.

Carl's company offered him an early retirement. He took it. He spends his days woodworking, which the engineer part of his mind adapted to quickly. He built a little workshop in the back of the property and creates furniture and lovely pieces of art.

I was, as is my nature, not able to sit in an office for too long. I quit and began to write travel books, easy to read books for travelers. The first being what to see and do in France and what not to see and do in France. Surprisingly, it sold very well. So, well that the publisher asked me to do one on Italy and Great Britain.

Today, I sit in front of my computer and look out my window. I look at Carl sitting on the deck reading the paper and drinking his coffee.

I think back and I am filled with love and gratitude that he was and is, and always will be, in my life.

We still take our walks. We still talk and share our thoughts, and now our many memories.

Then there are the moments, when I look back and I see the scruffy, little girl approach that shy, little boy. It's in those moments that I feel the joy that life can bring.

 A Letter

August 29, 1944
England

Hiya Folks,

Received you letter the other day and having a little time will try and answer it.

So you think that if this war lasts much longer that all of the Wodarskis will be gone. Wich way do you mean it, knocked off or just drafted? After this war blows over, we will all get together and as sure as your alive raise plenty of hell.

Well, what do you think of Chester being drafted just before they passed the new law? Him 37 years old and with a kid too. By the way, who is going to take care of Marieann now for him?

Glad to hear that you are coming along swell after your operation. How is Helen? Is she still working? Is she still holding on to the beer & some old wine she all ways had for me? Tell her it better be good and cold. We don't get ice cold beer like we did back home. Still am staying away from whiskey for some reason or other. I "cawn't" get used to it. So it looks like I am still the only Wodarski that doesn't or shall I say "cawn't" drink much.

Sorry to be writing this poor letter in pencil but my fountain pen has a funny habit of walking off for a couple of days.

Will close now. Wishing the both of you the best of luck.

Your Bro
Rudy

1984

Ed folded the letter and put it back in the tattered envelope as he did every September 10th for the last forty years. The tattered envelope that also held his brother's Mass card which said:

He who made the supreme sacrifice
for his country in France~
September 10, 1944

Ed, as always, when he read this letter, could hear the Glenn Miller Orchestra playing in the background. It was always *In the Mood*—one of Rudy's favorite songs. As always, he could see his brother's broad smile and handsome face. As always, he could feel the pain and loss.

He wiped away a tear, put the letter back in the little brown box that held pictures of Rudy and his other brothers.

"I'll see you soon, Bro," he said looking at the young soldier's black and white photograph. "And we'll have that cold beer."

 The Truth

Remnants, Sharon thought as she looked around the table at these people. *It's not chipped ceramics and aged photographs. It's people, these people. These are the remnants, the fragments of my past.*

It was a ninetieth birthday for Sharon's aunt, one of the last in person vestiges of the old neighborhood. A woman disliked by these people when they were children, but now the subject of stories and laughter.

Sharon feigned laughter and interest, but she didn't want to be here. Not with these people who reveled in their recollections of long-gone decades.

"Were you the one that hit me in the head with a rock?" someone asked Jack, who was sitting at her right. Jack being the main reason that Sharon didn't want to be here.

"What? No. What are you talking about?" Jack replied, wide-eyed.

The voices of the old friends all piped in.

"Jack, you hit her in the head with a rock?" someone asked.

"Whoa, this has got to be a good one." someone else commented with a laugh.

"Please explain what you just said," Jack uttered. "They'll all think I'm some kind of monster."

"I was about five," someone said, recalling a snowball fight decades earlier.

"Well, one of these snowballs had a rock in it and it hit me in the head. Enough for blood to flow and for me to get hysterical. My brother was furious," she continued. "He made every threat he could think of. He was supposed to be watching out for me and now he was in trouble."

"Excuse me, but that wasn't me!" Jack spoke up. "I'd never do that. Probably crazy Eddie. He was always doing shit like that."

Sharon sipped her drink, smiled politely and continued to block out the laughter and the conversation. She hoped it wouldn't turn in her direction, but of course it did.

"So, Sharon, how's your brother Joe doing?"

"He's fine. Living in Colorado with his wife. He just retired from the forestry service. He's doing good."

"And what about you, after all these years?" another someone asked.

"Yes, Sharon, where are you living now?" someone else asked. Sharon wished she could remember her name and if they were friends as children.

"North Lake Shore Drive. I have a condo."

"Really. Wow. Married?"

"Single, never married," she said stiffly, "worked in the financial markets and did well. Retired from all of that now."

No one said anything, but before long they began to talk among themselves. Then one of the men said:

"But now, Jack," someone else said. "you really did good. A best-selling novelist. Congratulations."

The others muttered their comments. Sharon's stomach clenched.

"You really cashed in on the old neighborhood, didn't you Jack?" Sharon said.

"I wouldn't put it that way."

"I googled your name, and the awards and accolades took up a whole page, not to mention having a New York Times best seller," Sharon continued, feeling the effects of the second martini that she just finished. "You did really good by all those crusty old immigrants and drunks. A real treasure trove of characters."

"Not all the stories take place there," Jack said, feeling the need to defend himself. "The short stories take place in New York, Italy, even Poland."

"Yeah, I know. I read them all," Sharon replied, looking straight ahead and not at him.

"I miss that old neighborhood," someone said.

"Yeah, me too," said another.

"I don't," Sharon tersely added. "I hated it."

"What? Really?" someone said.

"What was there to love? We owned a tavern and lived in that crummy apartment upstairs. Hotter than hell in the summer and just a space heater in the winter. One bathroom. My brother had to sleep on a sofa bed when I got older and when we couldn't share a room anymore. I had to put up with the racket from the tavern on weekend nights. Then there were the nights the cops would show up to break up a fight."

"Well, no one was rich. We were all kind of in the same boat. There were good times," said one.

"Yeah," Sharon sniffed derisively. "Like going to church every day and putting up with the nuns and priests."

"I was so jealous of those kids in other neighborhoods that lived in brick bungalows, especially the newer blond bungalows," Sharon continued. "I can remember seeing a swing set once in a back yard of one of those houses as we drove by. I couldn't believe it was possible for kids to have their own swing set."

"We had the park. That was better," someone interjected.

"Yeah, right. Just as long as you stayed away from the gangs," Sharon replied.

"Well, we all have our different memories," someone said. "Mine were good."

She let the others talk. She knew she said too much. One doesn't disrespect the old neighborhood. And she knew critical eyes were on her and it was best to stop talking.

She wondered if any of them remembered—they must. It was the talk for a long time. Someone was bound to bring it up, if not to her, then to each other as soon as they were away from the table.

As the conversation at the table drifted to other subjects, as if reading her mind, Jack said to her, softly but firmly, "I want you to tell me what happened."

"What?"

"That night. I want you to tell me what happened."

Sharon paled.

"Jack, it was decades ago. Why bring it up, especially at my aunt's party."

"Because all these years, you've avoided me. I tried to stay in touch, but you weren't having it."

"That's not true. I've seen you over the years."

"At two weddings and three funerals. And each time you did your best to steer clear of me. That's not going to happen tonight."

Sharon took a sip from her drink.

"Why are you doing this, Jack? It was so long ago."

Jack could hear the tension in her voice.

"I need to know, Sharon. I just need to know."

Sharon remained silent.

"He was my brother, god damn it," he continued. "I need to know the truth."

The others at the table looked over at them. The food was being served and the attention, gratefully for Sharon, was diverted.

"When this party is over, we're going to the bar downstairs, just you and me, and you're going to tell me what happened," he said faintly, but firmly. "Don't think about slipping out. I plan on being at your side all afternoon."

Sharon said nothing. Despite his words, she picked at her food and tried to work out an escape route.

As the party came to a close and phone numbers and email addresses were being exchanged, Jack took Sharon's arm and led her out of the banquet room and to the hotel bar.

"Enough already. I'm going," she said as she brushed away his hand. She had a lot to drink and little to eat. It was an effort to steady herself as they walked out.

"This will get the tongues wagging, Jack."

"Don't care," he replied, grabbing her arm again.

Although her head was reeling, her heart was racing.

Once seated at a booth, Jack went to the bar and came back with two ginger ales.

"What's this?"

"I want you reasonably sober when you start talking."

"For Christ's sake, Jack."

He stared at her so intently, she had to look away.

"I'm waiting," he said.

"Just like that. No small talk?"

His uninterrupted gaze frightened her.

"What makes you think you don't already know the truth," she said.

No response.

She looked Tom's brother in the eye.

"I loved him, Jack. I loved him so much. He was the love of my life."

"I know. So, what the hell happened that night?"

1968

Sharon walked over to the stereo and flipped the Simon and Garfunkel album to the other side and began to sing along with them.

"*I hear the drizzle of the rain,*" she sang off key.

"Stop already," her brother Joe barked. "It's enough I have to listen to this, you don't have to pipe in. And I am trying to study."

Sharon continued to sing until he threw a pen at her.

"Can't help it. I love this song."

"You've played this album twice already. Can you please put something else on? Put on the Hendrix album or the Doors."

"Ugh. But okay, after this song."

She looked over at her brother. "Do you remember that Leslie Gore song from a couple of years ago.

"How could I forget. That was another one you never stopped singing."

"There is a line that says:

"*I'm young and I love to be young. I'm free and I love to be free. To live my life the way that I want. To say and do whatever I please.*"

"That's how I feel, Joe. I just want to be free. I want to start living my life. I want a car and most of all I want my own place. My own apartment far away from this crummy neighborhood," she said.

Sharon liked these times with her brother, even if he didn't share her musical tastes and had to study—it was times like this when they talked to each other without their parents or friends around.

"Do ma and dad know you want to run off as soon as you can?"

"No. Of course not. All ma keeps telling me to do is get a job at a bank as soon as I graduate. Forget about college. Which isn't fair since you're going to college."

"They can't afford to send us both. You know that."

"She told me I could go to night school once a I have a full-time job. Hooray. And I should work on my typing and steno."

"What's wrong with that?"

"Nothing, but it's not for me."

"What is?"

"I don't know. I just know I don't want to be someone's secretary. I'd rather be the one with the secretary."

Her brother looked up from his book.

"That's pretty ambitious."

"Yeah, I know. Can't believe it came out of my mouth," she said. "I guess I just want more than other girls. Maybe I'm nuts."

"You're not nuts. Just smart. Your grades are always good, especially math. You're really good with numbers. Ma's right. You should go to night school and take some accounting classes. But get a job first."

"That's probably what I'll end up doing. What choice do I have?"

"Graduation is just a couple of weeks away and your birthday is what, three months away. You don't have to hang on for too much longer. And get a boyfriend, for Pete's sake."

"Like that's so easy. Even my girlfriends think I'm kind of weird. They can't wait to get married and pregnant. I can. And who am I going to meet around here. I can wait until I move away, hopefully to the north side. I'm sure I'll have a better chance of meeting someone that I have something in common with up there."

"Hmm, I'm not so sure about that."

"What do you mean?"

"Remember Jack and his brother Tom?"

"Bartkowski, something like that? Their dad's a big customer downstairs. Isn't he a plumber or something? I haven't seen them since we were kids. I wouldn't know either of them today."

"Yeah, that's them."

"One of them is a cop. Right?"

"Yeah, Jack's the cop. But Tommy, well he goes to school with me. We ride the same bus and started hanging around between classes. He's a good guy."

"Yeah, so?"

"I may live to regret this, but I think you would like him."

"Why do you think that?"

"To begin with, he has long hair- not real long but long enough."

"No crew cut or greased back hair. That's good, especially for this neighborhood. Your age?"

"We're a couple of months apart, so yes he's almost two years older than you." Joe replied. "He's not sure what he wants to do but he's taking a lot of science classes and says he might go into something medical."

"And why are you telling me this?"

"Do you want to get together with him? We can meet for pizza or something."

"I hate getting fixed up. It's always a disaster."

"Yeah, well I'm not crazy about it either, but I keep thinking that you two would hit it off. He even likes folk music and goes to coffee houses on the north side."

"And" he continued. "I'm a guy and I shouldn't probably be saying this, but he's what you girls would call cute and real hot, a fox."

"Hmm. You're not making this up so that I'll end up talking to some weirdo, while you take off laughing."

"You know me better than that. Ain't I the one who always looked after you, ever since you were real little."

"Yeah, I admit it. You are a very good big brother. Okay, but it has to be someplace real public and you have to be there and we have to have a code in case I hate him and want to leave."

"Right. Now I have to talk him into it."

Sharon didn't need the code. Once Sharon and Joe walked into the pizza parlor and sat down across from Tom, Sharon knew there would be no code.

After that evening, Sharon's friends became a sounding board for all the wonderful things about Tom.

"I'm smitten," she told them over lunch at school.

"Smitten? What's that supposed to mean?" Brenda asked.

"You could tell she likes her English class," said Karen.

"It means I am madly in love."

"Oh geez. You had three dates." Brenda said trying to hide a streak of jealousy. "Calm down."

"And we talk on the phone every day, sometimes twice a day. He's so fine. I can't wait for you guys to meet him. He's gorgeous and smart and loves all kinds of music."

"So, is he smitten?"

"Yes, he is. His gorgeous brown eyes kind of light up when he looks at me. Oh, girls, I have a boyfriend. A real boyfriend. He's a doll."

"Have your parents met him?" Karen asked.

"They know his mom and dad and knew him and his brother since they were little. So, yeah, they like him."

"Has he tried to get in your pants yet?" Brenda said, frowning.

"What! Brenda, we just went on three dates."

"Are you making out?" Karen piped in.

"Yes. Of course. That's what couples do."

"What are you going to do when he starts heading for third base, then a homerun?" Brenda added. "Has he mentioned the drive-in yet? That's usually when it happens."

"Brenda. Stop it. That's personal between Tommy and me."

"Won't be when you end up knocked up," Karen said.

"Yeah. Or else, after you put out, they're done with you," Brenda added. "They dump you. That's what happened with me and Chuck. What a jerk he was. And I fell for it. I thought he loved me too. I'm just glad that I didn't get knocked up."

"Geez, I thought you girls would be happy for me."

"We are, Sharon," Karen said. "Just be careful. Sounds like you're falling hard for this guy."

"I am and I know he feels the same about me. I'm not stupid. You'll see when you meet him. He's the best."

Sharon couldn't admit to her friends that she had these concerns. The one time that they had sex education at school, the nuns made a point of saying that sex was solely for marriage and to make babies. A good man who really loves you will wait until marriage, they told the class. If you're not married the others will use you for sex and toss you aside afterwards.

Tom wouldn't break up with her after having sex. She couldn't believe that of him. Or would he break up with her because she wouldn't have sex with him? The whole subject scared her. And she also knew that she knew next to nothing about sex and how to please a man. This too was never discussed in the sex education class. It sounded more like a biology class. It was sex, not the romantic love making that she had heard about in songs and what was hinted at in the movies.

She didn't know who to ask, certainly not her mother. And after the conversation with her friends, not them. And it wasn't like you could go to the library and ask for a book about it.

She prayed that when the time came, and she knew it would, that it would be worth the wait.

The days and nights sped by for Sharon. Graduation came and went. She began looking for a full-time job. The feeling of independence coupled with her time with Tommy made her happier than she had ever been. He was studying for his year-end tests and had gotten a job at a drug store near his house. It wasn't long before she went for her first interview and got hired by a large downtown bank near the Board of Trade building on LaSalle street.

An apartment was still a part of her plans, made even more important because of Tommy. A place for them, for privacy.

The subject of sex loomed on her mind and now in her body. Their times together, especially at the end of a date were becoming more intense, more intimate. She knew she was leaving him frustrated, but it seemed to her that he didn't want to talk about it anymore than she did.

But she knew he loved her. He bought himself a guitar and part of his graduation present to her was music. He learned how to play Love Me Do by the Beatles and played and sang it for her at her graduation party in front of all her friends and family.

The summer became weekends of sun-soaked beaches and rock concerts. There was always a group to see, new ones or established big stars.

The world was in tumult. The changes came fast and furious. Days came with violent headlines. Revolution was in the air. The Beatles sang about it. Music became the counterculture. There was the Vietnam War, Civil Rights, Women's Lib.

Sharon and Tom were caught up in the dialogue and the attitudes. His hair got longer and she at times shed her bra. The excitement of it all thrilled Sharon. Neither experimented with drugs. Tom had a good friend who overdosed. His body was found in the attic of his home by his father on a hot summer day.

Their attachment intensified. More words of love exchanged. The topic came up more than once.

"I'm afraid I'll get pregnant," she told him on the phone one late night.

"The pill is out there now."

"And just how do I get it? Ask my mother?"

"There are underground papers that have the information. We'll get our hands on one of them. You can get them at some clinics on the North Side."

"Fine. But then where? No more in the back seat of your little VW. Or hoping my parents or brother aren't at home. No, it has to be right. There is only one first time. It has to be special and memorable."

Tom let out a long sigh.

"Fine. Let's get the pill first and take it from there."

Sharon sensed his impatience.

"You understand, don't you Tom? Don't you?"

"Yes, I understand. But this is getting, well just frustrating. You know."

"I know that Tom. Not much longer. I promise. Hang in there. I want to do this with you. I really do. It just has to be right. We can't end up with a baby."

"I get it. I get it. I have to go. Or I'll be late for work. See you later."

"Yeah, see you later."

"I love you, Tom."

"Love you too, Sharon."

"Really truly?"

"Really truly." With relief she could hear the smile in his voice.

After she hung up, she called Brenda. Brenda would know and she did.

A few days later they drove to a women's clinic on the north side. A couple of hours later, Sharon had her pills. They drove back in silence, Sharon caught up in what was next.

That evening, when Tom picked her up, he could see her excitement.

"What's up?" he asked when she got in the car.

"I have something to tell you that will make you one happy man."

"And what would that be."

She took the pill container from her purse.

"I am officially on the pill."

His face brightened.

"You're kidding."

"Nope. Are you glad?"

"Yeah, real glad. Yeah. Okay, but now what?" he asked.

"As you know," she said lightly, "next Saturday is my eighteenth birthday. I know my parents will want to do something, but we can do it on Friday. I'll tell her that Brenda and some of the girls are going up to her aunt's place in Michigan to celebrate. I've gone up there before with Brenda and I'm sure she'll cover for me. I'll tell them we're going up on Saturday and will be back on Sunday."

"Besides," she continued, "I'll be eighteen and they can't stop me anymore. In a couple of months, I'll start looking for my own place. I'm so excited I could burst."

Tom ran his fingers through her hair and kissed her softly.

"You're wonderful, Shar, and I do love you."

"I love you to Tom. So much. I want so much to wake up in your arms the next morning."

She kissed him back.

"Now. Back to the details," she said. "Where will we go?"

"Let's get out of this city. We'll drive out to the country. Maybe a cabin or a motel somewhere. I'll think about it between now and then. It'll be great, babe. Just the two of us together, no friends or family or anyone we know. Just us."

"I can't wait, Tommy. A new beginning for me, for us. It's going to be wonderful."

"It was awful," Sharon said, wiping her hair away from her face.

"What was?" Jack asked.

"Everything. All of it. Tom had to work, and we left later then we wanted to, in the evening. The place he heard about that was going to be so romantic turned out to be an old cheesy run-down motel. I'm not sure how he found it, but it was far from what I had imagined. I tried to hide my disappointment and focus on the reason we were there.

"Ever the sophisticates, that we thought we were, Tom brought vodka and limes for Vodka Gimlets. I brought cheese and crackers, for midnight snacks. Dinner would be at a really nice restaurant, or so I thought.

I doubt that there was a nice place around there to eat. So, we were drinking vodka on pretty much empty stomachs."

"But Tom focused on why we were there."

She stopped talking.

"Go on," Jack prodded.

"I need a drink, a strong drink if you want the truth, Jack."

He went over to the bar and came back with two Vodka Gimlets.

"You do believe in hitting where it hurts, Jack. I haven't touched vodka since then."

Jack remained silent.

She took a sip and looked away. She didn't want to meet Jack's gaze.

"We started in on the vodka. I think we both wanted to hide our nervousness. I know I did."

"So, what else was awful?"

"The sex. The sex was awful. I didn't know what to expect. No one ever really told me. We were drunk. We fumbled and giggled. I didn't know that it would hurt so much and that I would bleed. It was so far from the romantic illusions that I had from movies and romance novels. Where was the so-called ecstasy? The stars, the beautiful threshold that I was crossing.

"Instead, there was grunting and grabbing and pain and blood. I hated it. I cried when he was done, and it was far from tears of joy."

"He seemed pleased. He was grinning when he rolled off of me. Sweaty and grinning," Sharon said softly, now on autopilot caught up in the memory.

"I was disappointed, beyond disappointed. I was angry. I ran in the bathroom and began to clean myself up. How should I put it, Jack? I was grossed out. Grossed out by the tiny bathroom, by the shabby room, by what I was wiping from my body. I came out yelling about how awful it all was. I drank some vodka out of the bottle.

"I told him I wanted to go home. That this was a disaster. I said some bad things."

"How did he react?'

"Shocked, I think. He wasn't expecting this kind of reaction. He said it would be better the next time. He told me to calm down. I didn't want to calm down. I wanted to get out of there. He seemed like a different person to me now. He wasn't my sweet, gentle Tommy.

"I started to get dressed. I didn't want him to see me naked. I didn't want to see him naked. He was trying to stop me from getting dressed. He was getting mad. Then I said it."

"Said what?"

She looked Jack in the eye.

"I told him he didn't know what he was doing. He was a lousy lover. I used those words—lousy lover."

"Then what?"

She breathed a deep sigh.

"He hit me. He slapped me in the face so hard I landed on the floor."

Jack's eyes widened but he said nothing.

"I was so stunned. He realized what he had just done and started to say something. I didn't hear what he said—my ears were ringing. I stood up, staggered actually and grabbed my purse and his car keys off the dresser and ran out of the room. Part of me was afraid of him and part of me was just plain angry."

She stopped long enough to take a drink, her narrative now coming at a faster clip.

"I got in the car and sped out of the parking lot. I had my license, but I didn't have a lot of driving experience. I took Drivers Ed and sometimes drove my dad's car, but I wasn't much of a driver. And I was crying. Plus, I had all that vodka in me.

"I turned on to the road, not knowing where I was even going. It was late and there were no other cars. I was swerving. I was going fast. I didn't see him."

"See who?'

"The hitchhiker. The kid in the flannel shirt with the long hair and a stubbly beard. Suddenly he was on the windshield then flipped over and was gone.

"I slammed on the brakes. A hallucination, I thought. That didn't happen. I got out of the car, still believing it didn't happen. But it did. He was laying on the side of the road, his legs in different directions, his face contorted, his eyes open.

"I backed away and wanted to scream. I had my fist in my mouth. There's no logic at a time like that. I actually wondered who did this to him. Reality started to click in. I wasn't that far from the motel and began running toward it. I needed Tommy. Tommy will fix this.

"As it turned out, he tried chasing the car, then he heard the tires screech. He was running in my direction when I saw him.

"I remember I tried to wake him up. Tommy was yelling at me to stop—that he wouldn't wake up. A car came by and Tommy waved them down and someone said something about getting the police."

She stopped talking.

Jack was unable to speak.

She finally broke the silence.

"Tommy said to go along with what he would tell the cops, that I shouldn't say anything, only agree with what he was saying. It's an accident, he said. The cops will see that. He made me promise. I promised. I would have promised anything to anyone at that point. I just wanted to step out of that reality.

"The cops who showed up, well, they were small time cops, rude and nasty. Called us lousy hippies. Said we were probably on drugs. Coming in from the big city, thinking they could do what they wanted. I couldn't stop crying.

"And then I heard Tommy. I heard him say, I heard him say that he was driving. I stopped crying and tried to say something. He looked over at me and repeated it. *I was driving. It was an accident. He stepped in front of the car. An accident. Yes, I had a drink with my girlfriend. We went out to get something to eat. Yes, it's my car. Here's my license.*

"I think he was really surprised when they put handcuffs on him. I was. I started to say something. I tried to run over to him, but a cop was holding me back. I heard the words vehicular manslaughter.

"That's when he looked over at me. I'll never forget his expression. Call Jack he screamed at me. Call Jack.

"One of the cops snickered and said that he hoped Jack was a good lawyer because Tom was going to need one. Another cop took me back to the motel and I called you."

A spasm ran through Sharon's body. She couldn't look up at Jack, not yet. She heard him take a deep breath. He rattled the ice in his glass.

"I remember that call." he finally said. "I don't think I've ever forgotten a word that you said to me on that call."

"Did you ever tell anyone?" he added.

"Joe. Joe knew. I had to tell someone. It was months later. Our relationship was never the same. I would see him looking at me, then shake his head or leave the room. We still talk, but rarely and it's not like it should be, even after all these years."

The sound of laughter coming from another table rattled Sharon. She looked over at them praying that they would go away.

Then she looked at Jack. The eyes. Tommy and Jack always resembled each other, mostly in the eyes. She could see what Tom would have looked like after all these years.

"I always knew," he said calmly. "Tom never said. But I knew. I just had to hear it from you."

"How did you know?"

"The day in court when he was sentenced. You were sitting next to me. You mumbled—it should be me. It should be me. You said it one other time."

"At the wake."

"Yes, at the wake. I don't think anyone else heard or made the connection or wanted to for that matter."

"It was my mantra for days, months, years, and now decades."

"Tell me about your life since then," he said.

"Why?"

"Just curious. How did you live with this all these years?"

"Live? I existed. I threw myself in work. I did go to night school and learned about financing. It wasn't long before I ended up at the Board of Trade. I had a friend who worked there, and she got me in. I started out as a runner and ended up in the back room of a brokerage firm. Ended up managing the office. Went to another company and managed that office. Worked a lot of hours, but I didn't care. I ended up with my own seat on the Exchange. Made a lot of money. Bought a condo on Lake Shore Drive. Retired fairly young and traveled around a lot. Got bored and did consulting work."

"And never married?"

"Yeah right, marriage," she snickered. "A few relationships that amounted to nothing because that's how I wanted it. Had lovers, usually married men. I was poison. I didn't deserve to be happy. There was this horrible secret that I couldn't tell a soul. If I did tell someone, they would hate me, like Joe does to this day. And now I'm sure you do."

He didn't respond.

"And what about you?" she asked. "How did you get through this? Seems like you did okay."

"Really. Is that how it seems to you?" he said sardonically.

Sharon shrugged.

"I was a cop for only three years when I got your call. I quit six years later—a week after Tommy got killed by some deviant pig in that prison cell block. Tom always thought that since I was a cop it would help. It didn't. The folks wanted to know who we could bribe. Of course, we could bribe someone. Turns out we couldn't. The incident took place outside of Chicago. That's how crazy our conversations were.

"There was next to nothing that I could do to help my kid brother. It tore me up. I was actually afraid it would make things worse for him once he got in jail if they knew his brother was a cop. He was counting on me and I let him down. All I could do was get him a lawyer and sit back like everyone else and hope for the best.

"I was married with a kid on the way the night of the accident. I know this messed up my marriage. Six years later I'm an ex-cop with two kids. Linda, my ex, was a lawyer, so she had the income to support us when I quit. I stayed home with the kids. I did some security work, mainly to get out of the house. Took some night classes, began writing. My first book, to everyone's surprise, especially mine, became a best seller. The rest is history, as they say.

"And there was the divorce. I turned out to be a lousy husband. Moody and distant. Tommy was always on my mind. I visited him just about every week, even missing some of my kid's events. What ate at me was the injustice of it all. I saw rich kids from the North suburbs who did worse and got little or no sentences. The big-time lawyers and rich parents padded their way out of jail. It made me sick. It made me mad and it made me a bad cop. I had to get out."

"You didn't let him down. He idolized you."

"Yeah, sure. You didn't see the anger and frustration when I went to visit him. His life was hell in that place. He begged me to get him out, even a different jail. There wasn't a damn thing that I could do. Maybe if I had some seniority, but I was just some beat cop. His lawyer was useless.

"A ten-year sentence," he continued, "it was too much. He was a good kid, no record, going to college. It was too long. The judge was a heartless bastard. The word accident meant nothing to him."

"And you," he said. "I knew that you weren't visiting him. What the hell was that all about?"

"He told me to stop coming. More than once he told me to stop coming and get on with my life. The more I protested, the more he insisted. He said it was too hard on him after I left. He didn't even want me to write, but I did. I never stopped doing that."

She added, "And I never stopped loving him, Jack."

She wiped away a tear, then called the server over and asked for another drink for the both of them.

"It was because he hit me. He said that was why I ended up doing what I did. He said it really was his fault. If he hadn't hit me, I wouldn't have run out and it would have never happened. He apologized to me from jail. How crazy was that? Him apologizing to me."

"In a way he was right," she continued. "At times, it was what got me through it all. That sounds terrible, but I grabbed at anything to help me cope."

"So how long did you live with your parents?" Jack asked.

"A couple of years. As it turned out, I needed them more than I thought I ever would. I was practically out of my mind when it happened. Somehow, they got me to eat and they got me pills so that I could sleep. The nightmares were horrible. I still have them."

"I moved downtown for a couple of reasons. The main one being that I didn't have to have a car. I can get around without one. I renew my license and occasionally rent a car if I really need to. But driving terrifies me, especially at night. I thought I would get past it, but I never did. I can still feel that thud. I can still see his body. Even after all these years."

"Who told you when Tom got killed. I know it wasn't me," Jack said.

"My parents came over to the apartment that I had on the north side. Once again, they took care of me."

For a few minutes, neither spoke, lost in their own thoughts.

"Guilt is a terrible thing, Jack," Sharon said. "It eats at you. It never lets you go. It can dominate you. I still remember going to visit Tom, even after he told me not to. He changed so much from my Tommy, my boyfriend, who took me to coffee houses and loved music, all music and read Hermann Hesse and the classics.

"The young man with the gentle brown eyes had hardened himself, even his voice sounded different. He looked at me with hatred in his eyes. That's really why I stopped going. I couldn't take the way he looked at me."

"He had to do that to survive in that place," Jack said. "Be as bad as they were. Although in the end, he wasn't bad enough."

"I did want to confess, Jack, I really did. He said no one would believe me. I'd be saying it just to get him out of jail. But it was because of me that he was there. It was because of me that he died. And I've had to live my whole life knowing that."

"He made the decision, Sharon. It was the wrong decision and he, and we, paid a price for that night."

"I've tried to put it behind me, but it rears its ugly head and always will," she said.

"You need to forgive yourself. I guess we both do."

"No, Jack. I can't. I won't. It's my punishment for my silence. My selfish silence. You know, a small part of me was always relieved that I didn't get caught. That sounds terrible especially saying it to you."

"I always wondered how I would feel hearing you tell me the truth," he said.

"And just how do you feel, Jack? Now that you know the truth."

He remained silent and sipped his drink.

He finally said,

"Sharon, I understand, I think that was all I wanted, to understand. It's hard to think about Tommy and me as kids and teenagers. We were close, real close. His memories were always tied up in tragedy. I think now I can remember my kid brother as he was, as we were. I'm glad I heard it all. I needed to."

"You don't despise me?"

"I don't have the emotional energy to despise you, Sharon. You've suffered enough. We both have. You don't need me coming down on you. Maybe it would have been different if I heard this twenty, thirty years ago. I was angrier back then.

"Now, well, I'm glad that I know the truth. I think that's all I ever needed, the truth, regardless of how hard it is to hear it. What's the saying—the truth will set you free."

"Thank you for making me tell you," Sharon replied. "I always wanted you to know. That's probably why I said those things when you were nearby. Part of me knew you would understand. No one else would. Joe didn't."

"What now?" Jack asked.

"Now I go back to my life as a well-off senior citizen who gives money to charities and travels to all corners of the world. I have pictures of me and Tommy from that summer, not a lot, but enough to make me go back in time. Sometimes I pull them out and think 'what if'. I like to think that we'd be married with kids and careers. Then I sob and put them away for another few years."

"And you, Jack?" she asked.

"I go back to peddling my books. Not sure I want to write anymore."

"You can write about your kid brother."

He paused and smiled.

"I may just do that, Sharon. I may just do that," he replied. "In the meantime, I guess we should head on home. It's been a hell of a day."

"Yes, it has, Jack. Yes, it has," Sharon said reaching for her purse. "And now it's time to go."

"Do you need a lift home?"

"No, actually I have a room here. I'll leave tomorrow. I'm a big Uber customer now."

"Jack," she said when they got to the lobby. "Keep in touch. Okay. I think I need that."

"I will, Sharon. You too. No more running from me."

She smiled.

"No more running, Jack. I promise, no more running."

She leaned in and kissed his cheek.

"You're a part of him for me," she said.

"And you're a part of him for me. You always will be."

She turned and headed for the bank of elevators.

He stood in the lobby and watched as she got on the elevator and the doors closed.

Then he walked out slowly into the cool fall evening.

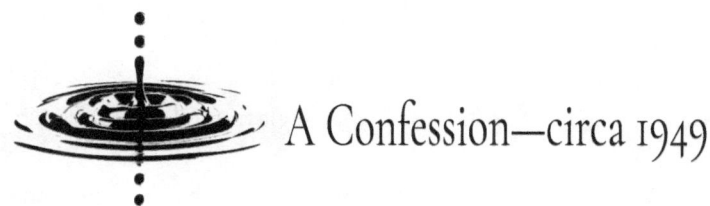 A Confession—circa 1949

"Bless me Father for I have sinned. It's been, ah, well, who the hell knows."

"Yes, um continue," the priest said from the other side of the grate.

"Is that you Harry?"

"Pardon me?"

"It's me, Harry. Stanley. Stanley Wincauskas."

"Mother of Mercy," The priest muttered.

"How ya doin, Harry?"

"It's Father Harold," the priest replied firmly. "And I'm fine, Stanley. But the confessional is hardly the place for a social visit."

"I can come see you at the rectory, if you want."

Heaven help me. The priest thought.

"No, no, that's quite alright. Just tell me what's on your mind. Begin your confession."

"Yeah, well, ah. I missed Sunday mass like for a long time. I cuss a lot and I like to gamble. Not sure if gambling's a sin, though. Tough on the wallet. Probably why I cuss so much and miss Sunday mass. Someone said I stole their car, but I just borrowed it for a Saturday night. It was Ted Zigmund's. He was a real asshole. Oops, there I go again with the cussing. Sorry Harr, er Father."

"Please continue," Father Harold said, anxious to get Stanley out of the confessional. Stanley was known around the neighborhood as Smelly Stoshu. He had a well-known aversion to bathing and this was apparent after just a few moments in the close quarters of the confessional.

"Anyway, I knocked up my girlfriend."

"What? Please repeat that."

"I knocked up my girlfriend."

"Isn't your girlfriend, Ursula? The girl who cleans and cooks for us at the rectory."

"Yep. That's the one. My little Ursula ain't real happy right now. Knocking up a girlfriend ain't a sin, is it?"

"No, No. I guess it's not. It's what happens now that's important," The priest responded, obviously flustered. "Sex is meant for marriage. You know that Stanley. I'm sure Ursula knows that as well."

"That's easier said than done, Father. I get cravings, you know. Well, you probably don't, seeing as you never had it. Don't know how you guys do it. I couldn't. Maybe that's why I ain't a priest."

The priest could hear him laugh.

"Stanley, you are going to do the right thing and get married. Aren't you?"

"That's why I'm here. I lied to Ursula and said I wanted to marry her. But I don't. I got no money. Can't support a wife and a kid."

"What are you doing for a living? Last I heard you were working at the stock yards."

"Quit that. I'm working at the liquor store over on 47th Street. Never want to see another cow or pig as long as I live. Don't care how much they pay me."

"You have a responsibility now Stanley. You're bringing a child into the world. A child that will need a good home with good Catholic parents who will look after his education as well as his soul."

Stanley said nothing.

"You can get a better job, get a nice little flat. She has a good family that will help out, I'm sure. Ursula can work for us for a short while, but she will have to leave once she begins to show. It wouldn't be appropriate. And she must be married Stanley. I hope you understand this."

"Yeah, I do. It's not just the money, Father."

"Then what's the problem?"

"She don't like me. She said so. I like her okay. She's cute and nice. When she found out she was knocked up, er with child, she said she could do better. I was fun but I would be a lousy husband and father."

"We are talking about the same Ursula that works at the rectory with all nine of us priests and goes to mass every Sunday and sometimes during the week."

"Yeah, go figure. You think you know someone, eh Father?"

Father Harold cleared his throat.

"You need to spend more time with her and convince her that it's not true. You can buckle down, give up the gambling. You can do this, Stanley. For the child and for Ursula, you must do this."

"Can you talk to her?"

"What?"

"I'll marry her, but I can't if she don't want to marry me. I kinda like the idea of having a kid."

The silence lasted long enough for Stanley to ask, "You still in there, Father? You didn't go and sneak out?"

The priest could hear Stanley laugh again.

"Okay, Stanley, this is what I'll do. I will meet with you and Ursula in the rectory. Let's say Monday at ten o'clock. I want you to look your best. You take a bath and wear a nice shirt and slacks. Do you understand? I want you to start thinking about getting a new job. You have to tell Ursula that you are looking hard for a decent job, and that you will stop gambling."

"Geez, Father. The gambling. Can't you just make me say a hundred rosaries on my knees or something?"

He laughed again.

"I'm serious, Stanley. This affects the rest of your life. Do you want another man to raise your child?"

"No, guess not. I wouldn't like that at all."

"I'll speak with Ursula when I get back to the rectory. I'll tell her that I know about the baby and I'll tell her about the meeting on Monday. I won't say anything else to her until our meeting on Monday."

"Okay, Father. I'll be there."

"You have to be there, Stanley."

"I will. I can't lie to a priest, now can I?"

"That's right. No lying to a priest. That is a sin."

The silence and the body odor increased.

"You can go now, Stanley."

"You didn't give me absolution."

"Oh, yes, of course."

The priest gave him absolution and blessed him. His penance was five Our Fathers to be said at mass the next day."

He heard a groan on the other side of grate.

"I'll see you on Monday. Don't be late."

"I won't. Ya know it's funny. You talk like an old man and you're just a couple of years older than me, Harry.

Stanley laughed again as he left the confessional. Harry laughed, too.

Three weeks later, Father Harold presided over the wedding of Stanley and Ursula Wincauskas.

Seven months later he baptized their son.

Twenty-five years later he presided over their twenty fifth wedding anniversary mass.

Twenty-five years after that he presided over their fiftieth wedding anniversary mass.

Ursula and Stanley held hands during Father Harold's funeral.

# November Gray

I hate days like this. Gray, cold, damp. Especially the damp. Hate the damp. Makes my arm hurt. When my arm hurts, I have to push away the reason why my arm hurts.

Sometimes I can't. Like today.

It was the same kind of weather. November weather. Hideous month. To me November is a mistake. Too late for the colors of October and too early for the sheer, clean whiteness of December. A mistake. November is the month that celebrates dead war veterans and a president's assassination. To me, an awful month. And don't get me started on Thanksgiving. What if you have nothing to be thankful for?

I was only six. That in itself seems remarkable. Six is so young. Too young to be damaged. I loved school and my little friends. And I always came home right after school. I didn't want to worry Mommy, since she said I was a big girl and could walk the block and a half to school by myself.

I walked into the kitchen of our flat. We lived on the first floor. Grammy and Papa lived upstairs.

Daddy was there, slouched at the kitchen table, instead of being at work. He had a glass of whisky in front of him. He did that on Saturdays. Not on school days. I couldn't understand why he was home and drinking whiskey.

"Hi Daddy." I said as I took off my coat and woolen hat. I hung them up on the peg by the door, like Mommy wanted me to do.

"Hi, Daddy," I said again since he didn't answer the first time.

"I ain't your Daddy."

"Huh?" I didn't understand what he said.

"I ain't your god-damned Daddy." He snarled at me like a mean dog.

I couldn't say anything because I didn't understand what he meant. He was always my Daddy. How could he not be my Daddy anymore? And he said a bad word. I began to get scared. I didn't move. I just stared at him.

"What the hell you staring at? Didn't you hear me?" He hollered at me. "Turns out I'm not your Daddy. I'm a nothing. That lousy slut of a mother was lying to me all these years."

I looked around the kitchen, wishing Mommy would walk in and help me.

"I bet you didn't even know that. Did you?" He looked even more like a mean dog now. His eyes were so red.

I started to edge my way out of the room.

"Where do you think you're going, you little bastard."

I was scared. This wasn't my Daddy. He even said so. I didn't know who he was, but he wasn't my Daddy.

When I started to walk away, he grabbed me by my left arm and squeezed.

"You don't even look like me."

"Daddy," I mumbled, so afraid.

"Don't you ever call me Daddy!" he shouted. "I'm not your Daddy!"

With that, he yanked my arm so hard, I screamed. Then he threw me across the room. I felt it as it broke. I screamed in pain and fear. Where was Mommy? I thought. Mommy should come and save me.

The mean dog was over me now, breathing heavily, with spit falling from his mouth. He screamed at me to shut up. Shut up! He kept screaming.

"Shut the fuck up!" he screamed.

I couldn't. The pain in my arm was so awful and I was so afraid.

I felt his huge hands around my neck and the pressure on my throat. That was all I remember. It went dark.

When I woke up, I saw my Grammy's face. She was crying but smiled when she saw I was awake. My arm was in a big cast and everything looked funny.

"Grammy?"

"Oh, Lucy, baby, you're awake. I was so scared."

"Mommy?"

My mouth felt funny. That was all I could say.

"It's gonna be okay, baby," Grammy said. "I'll take care of you, baby. It's gonna be alright. Everything is going to be fine."

Grammy cried even more. I felt too funny to wonder what was happening and went back to sleep.

It was days later when I was able to go home. Not to my flat, not to my bedroom, but to Grammy and Papa's flat.

I found out later, much later, that Grammy heard my screams and ran downstairs. She saw my father over me, with his hands on my neck and screaming at me to shut up. There was a frying pan on the stove. She hit him on the head until she knocked him out.

She called the police and then she called Papa, who was at work.

Then my Grammy walked into the bedroom, where she found my mother's lifeless body.

 Afterwards

Truth be told, he was a lousy husband. Joyce wrote in response to a condolence letter that she received when her husband passed away.

Irresponsible, selfish, lazy, liked to party—a lousy lover, a brute. She wrote with a grin.

She knew she wouldn't mail it, but it felt good to write it. He was that and more.

She went through the motions of a grieving widow for all to see. Privately, she felt relief. She also felt liberated after 23 years of marriage.

Thinking back to her wedding day, she wondered out loud—*What planet was I on?*

Was I so desperate for love and security that I married the first man that came along?

She answered loudly to the empty room. Yes. Yes, I was.

This is what happens when you spend eight of your first eighteen years in foster care, she thought. *This is what happens when your parents die in a car accident on the way to pick you up from summer camp, and you are but a child. This is what happens when the few relatives that you have run in the other direction when the agencies come looking for someone to take you in.*

Joyce tore up the letter.

She walked around the small living room of her home and wondered, what now? Despite all of Leroy's shortcomings, he did provide. As a car mechanic he made decent money. The house was paid off and there were no outstanding bills. The insurance paid for the funeral and left a little beyond that. There was a decent size savings account and a couple of CDs. Financially, Joyce felt secure.

Emotionally, Joyce felt bereft. The few in-laws that they had on Leroy's side were replicas of Leroy. If she never saw any of them again, she was fine with that. It was the nieces and nephews that she was drawn to when they were children. But as in life, they grew up and became adults that scattered to different locations, not bothering to give Leroy and Joyce their addresses.

They had no children. Joyce yearned for a child, but Leroy wouldn't go for the tests that the doctor recommended, saying it was obvious that the problem was with Joyce. She had a lousy womb or something, he would tell people.

Joyce worked for years at the local supermarket, first as a cashier then as a supervisor. She was a fixture there and in town. She had a number of acquaintances, but no close friends. Leroy didn't want people, other than his drinking and sports enthusiast buddies, stopping in at the house. And he didn't allow Joyce to spend too much time on the phone.

Allow. She thought. *I lived a life being allowed to do things. Never again. No one will ever do that to me again. I will never live under the word "allow" again.*

Without giving it much thought, Joyce dialed the number for the supermarket and asked to speak to Mr. Ridgeway, the manager. With 18 years of employment at the supermarket, she still referred to her boss as Mr. Ridgeway. Mr. Ridgeway, the Manager. Mr. Ridgeway, who corrected her loudly if she made a mistake. Mr. Ridgeway, who never held back from making a lewd remark or grabbing her behind with a grin that turned her stomach.

"Mr. Ridgeway," she said when he picked up the call. "It's Joyce."

"Joyce. How are you handling things?"

"I'm handling things just fine. The worst is over."

"I suppose it is. Did you get the flowers that we sent you? All the employees pitched in for them, you know."

"Yes, I got them. They're beautiful," she said looking at the drooping red roses in the cheap vase.

"So, when do you think you'll be back at work? We really need you around here."

"I won't be back, Mr. Ridgeway. I'm terminating my employment."

"What? Say again. I don't understand," he sputtered.

"Nothing to understand. I won't be returning. I quit," she said, thinking about how good it felt to say those words.

"I quit," she repeated.

"You can't just up and quit," he continued to sputter.

In her mind she could picture the saliva flying through the air, which was something that happened when he was upset.

"Yes, I can and yes, I am," she replied "You can get rid of whatever is in my locker. I won't be returning to pick any of that up."

"Joyce, that's just the grief talking. You know what they say—you shouldn't make big decisions at a time like this. Just calm down and think about what you're saying."

"I'm perfectly calm and I repeat, I quit. Thank you and goodbye, Mr. Ridgeway." She replied and hung up the phone.

She walked through all the rooms. When she got to the bedroom, she stopped, hands on her hips and looked around the small, neat, room.

My marital bed. What a joke. Glad I don't ever have to do that again, she thought. *I suppose I should start getting rid of his stuff.*

She looked at his dozens of sports tee shirts, all on hangers, and his mechanic's coveralls that she spent so many years trying to keep clean. She looked down at his dirty sneakers and slippers, and his worn robe that he wore for years while sitting in front of the television drinking beer.

She turned and headed for the basement and returned with the only suitcase that they ever owned. Leroy didn't like traveling and wouldn't allow her to. The suitcase was purchased when they had to leave town—once for a wedding and twice for family funerals. It hadn't been used since.

She began filling the suitcase with her clothes, everything that would fit. When it was stuffed, she grabbed some grocery bags and filled them with some of the groceries from the cabinets. Another was filled with a few of her favorite books, cookbooks, and pie tins. She added a couple of photos of her parents and her baby pictures. Almost as an afterthought she threw in some paperwork that she thought she would need some day. Then she reached under the bed for one last item, surprised at how heavy it was.

It all got lugged out to the car. She hoped none of her nosier neighbors would stop and ask her what she was doing. If they did, it would be Leroy's things going to charity.

She felt nothing as she looked around the small house. There was nothing that meant anything to her—nothing that triggered a happy memory. She shrugged.

Joyce loved candles, the more fragrant the better. Leroy allowed this indulgence. She walked through the rooms and lit some candles—two or three in each room.

After enough candles were lit, she walked over to the stove and turned on all four burners, making sure that there were no flames.

Calmly, she took her purse and keys, got in the car and drove away.

Before she reached the edge of the town, she heard the explosion.

A smile lit up her face. The Willie Nelson song *On the Road Again* ran through her head even though she had never really been on the road before.

In the next town over she stopped at the bank and cleared out all but five dollars from her checking account. She did the same with one of her savings accounts.

Her last stop was Walgreens, where she picked up a Road Atlas, as well as a few bags of candy to snack on.

She drove on with no idea of where she was going and not caring.

She spent that first night in a motel chain over three hundred miles from where she had started. She was impressed by how large the room was and that a microwave, coffee maker and a small refrigerator was included. And then there was that free breakfast.

She decided to stay for two nights.

The time was spent watching television shows that she didn't know existed. The room had something called HBO and she took full advantage of what it offered.

She also studied her atlas and decided which direction to go.

South for sure, she thought. Somewhere warm where you never had to shovel snow again or endure twenty below zero wind chills. Somewhere like Arizona. She had known people who went there to escape the winters. She couldn't imagine what it must be like when it's seventy degrees in January. Arizona, yes, Arizona it is.

Joyce smiled and kept the atlas open to the Arizona page.

She took her time getting to Arizona. There were so many scenic overlooks to stop at, so many roads off the highway to explore. So many fellow travelers to chat with.

Joyce never felt so alive.

But Joyce was also realistic. The money would not last forever. Once she got to Arizona, she knew that she would have to find a place to settle down and get a job.

Would she be able to get a job, she worried? She gave no two-week notice, which was always a requirement. Mr. Ridgeway may not give her a good reference.

And then there was that little matter of blowing up her house. She knew that there must be a crime in there. The thought that an All-Points Bulletin, a term she heard on TV, would be issued for her made her laugh.

Sweet, quiet, churchgoing, model wife, blowing up her house made her laugh until she cried. She knew she was definitely the talk of that town now.

Once in Arizona, Joyce headed directly to Flagstaff. She made two trips to the Grand Canyon, making sure that she took it all in. Standing at the overlook, and seeing the people around her, mostly speaking in foreign languages, Joyce realized how much she had missed out on and vowed to never let that happen again.

From there she drove to Sedona and was as awestruck as the other travelers. Heading down to Phoenix, she saw the saguaro cactuses in the distance. She got off at the next exit so that she could walk among them.

From there it was down to Phoenix, where for the first time in her travels, she got lost, confused and flustered. She pulled over to a side street and took a deep breath.

This is more than I can handle. Too much traffic, too many buildings, too many people. I guess I'm a small-town girl after all. She said out loud as she headed back up north.

She took an exit almost halfway to Flagstaff hoping to find a place to stay for a couple of nights. Driving through a small town she spotted a motel. It looked like something out of the 1950's, worn but with some life left in it. This appealed to Joyce. It wasn't fancy. The lobby as well as the room still clung to the paneling and décor of the fifties and early sixties. There were none of the perks the other motels offered, but it felt warm, cozy and warm. It made Joyce smile. She booked a room for a week.

The staff was friendly and helpful. The owners, Mickey and Luanne were an older couple, and the second generation to run it, they told her. Even though it was a not a big money maker, they were not about to let it go. They made enough to survive. And it was a respectable place. There was still a tourist trade and enough old timers that like the old-fashioned look of the place.

When she asked about a place to eat, they directed her to a restaurant down the main road, walking distance from the motel, if she felt like a good walk.

Joyce did, in fact, feel like a good walk. The weather was picture perfect, with the bluest sky that she had ever seen. With her hands in her pockets she headed toward the restaurant.

She could see the faded sign come into view. The building had a worn wooden façade, which made it look like something out of the old west. The gravel parking lot was filled with cars, which to Joyce, indicated good food.

In her previous life, Joyce considered herself a shy person, but no longer. There was no hesitancy in chatting up whoever came her way. That would bother Leroy, she thought, but it also occurred to her that Leroy was rarely in her thoughts anymore.

In the restaurant, it was the waitress, whose name was Helen, that Joyce began a conversation with. The restaurant, being busy, kept Helen on her toes, but she found time for small talk with Joyce.

And the food was delicious—the best meat loaf Joyce ever had. When it was time for dessert, she asked for a suggestion.

"Well, we're really known for our homemade pies. That's why we have so many regular customers. But I don't know what we're going to do next week. Elsie, the lady who makes the pies, is quitting. Too hard on her, she says. She's getting up in years, she says, although I happen to know that she is still on this side of seventy. Acts like she's ninety-five. Do you want to try her apple crumble? It's one of the favorites?"

"Yes, of course, that sounds great," Joyce smiled.

She finished off the pie quickly.

It's a good slice of pie, but not as good as mine. Too much cinnamon, she thought, as she mulled over an idea.

Joyce was known in her town as the best pie maker around. She actually won a few blue ribbons at the state fair. Leroy would joke that it was the reason he married her. She always sold out first at the church bake sales.

She left a generous tip for Helen and made her way to the register to pay her bill. She asked the girl at the register if the manager were available and if she could talk to him—not make a complaint, just talk.

His name was Leo, and he came out of the kitchen wiping his hands on his apron. He was an older man, probably close in age to Mickey at the motel.

Joyce introduced herself and told him that she was planning on staying in the area.

He nodded and smiled.

"I understand that you'll be needing someone to make your pies. I want you to know that since I do plan on living in the area, I'll be looking for a job. And I also want you to know that I make really great pies. I've won awards."

"Is that at fact?"

"Yes, it is and I'm a very hard worker."

He nodded and told Joyce to have a seat at the counter.

He returned with a woman whom he introduced as Fannie, his wife and the other owner of the restaurant.

"Tell her what you told me," he said to Joyce. "I'll leave it up to her. She's a good judge of character."

"So," Fannie began, "Tell me what you told him."

Joyce told her about her late husband and the small town, omitting the explosion part. She told her about her job at the supermarket. There were unfortunately no children. She told Fannie how she loved Arizona and wanted to settle down there. It seemed that once she started talking, she couldn't stop.

Fannie nodded occasionally and let her talk.

"Tell me about your pies," Fannie finally interjected.

"I've been baking since I was little. Mostly pies. My grandmother taught me. I make all kinds—you name it—I can make it. Some are my own recipes. Those are the ones that won the Blue Ribbons."

"Okay, er Joyce, your name is Joyce, right?"

"Right."

"Here's what we'll do. You come in tomorrow at six and meet Elsie. She'll show you around and then you make a couple of your pies and we'll let you know if you have the job. Does that sound okay to you?"

"Yes, yes," Joyce said, reaching out to shake Fannie's hand. "That's more than fair. You won't be disappointed. I'll be here at six."

She was there at six and they were not disappointed in her pies. The job was hers. Joyce was beaming when she got back to the motel and told Mickey and Luanne. They seemed as thrilled as she was.

"Can I have the room for a month, until I find something else."

"Of course, you can," Luanne said, giving Joyce a big hug. "Stay as long as you need to."

Joyce couldn't remember a time in her life when she was happier.

It didn't take long for Joyce's pies to become one of the most popular items on the menu. Leo and Fannie decided to start selling whole pies. They set up a counter to the left of the doorway, even taking out a booth. They set up a new glass case and a second register. The whole pies sold as well as the slices in the restaurant. An article appeared in the local paper praising the pies. Fannie was soon called on to help with the piemaking tasks. After a couple of months, Leo gave Joyce a bonus and Fannie gave her a big hug and told her how happy they were that she stopped in that day.

Joyce found a little cottage to rent near the top of a hill that had views of the valley below, as well as stunning sunsets.

Without a doubt, she laughed, *the best thing Leroy ever did for me was to drop dead.*

Joyce loved the warm, early morning hours. Once the pies where done, she would sit at the picnic tables that Leo had set up to the side of the restaurant, drink her coffee, think about what pies she would make the next day and make a list of what she would need.

It was a morning such as this that a white truck pulled up in the empty lot across the road. A box truck, she recalled. Leroy worked on many of this type.

From the passenger side, a young girl stepped out. Joyce watched as the girl frowned, wiped her mouth and shoved something in her front pocket.

The truck pulled away. Joyce watched as it did.

Then she turned her attention to the girl. She was young, maybe fifteen or sixteen, possibly younger. Joyce hoped not. She wore a tight tee shirt without a bra and low riding jeans, and badly applied make-up. There were stripes of purple in her messed brown hair.

Joyce watched as she went inside the restaurant, then got up and followed her.

Aside from the pies, Leo recently started selling souvenirs—magnets, postcards, small shot glasses—all promoting Arizona.

Instead of going into the restaurant, the girl went into the bathroom.

When she left the bathroom, the girl began to browse the souvenirs. Joyce watched as she lifted a couple of magnets and two shot glasses and put them in her purse.

Joyce approached the girl from behind.

"You probably don't even have a refrigerator to put those magnets on," she said sternly to the girl.

The girl looked over her shoulder and frowned at Joyce.

"Put them back," Joyce ordered.

"Who the fuck are you? Some kinda cop. I'm gonna pay for them."

"Like hell you are and I'm not a cop, but I work here, and I know some cops who are having breakfast here right now. Shall I call them?"

The girl scowled and said nothing.

"Put them back," Joyce ordered again.

Glaring at Joyce, she put the items back.

"Have you had breakfast?" Joyce asked.

"Huh? What the fuck do you care?"

"I'll ask again. Have you had breakfast?"

"No."

"Fine, come with me."

"Where to? Your cop friends?"

"No, to go eat breakfast."

The girl hesitated and Joyce firmly took her arm and led her to a corner in the restaurant. After they were seated the girl crossed her arms and glared at Joyce.

"Order a hearty breakfast," Joyce ordered. "It's on me."

"Why? You fucking weirdo. Why should I let you buy me breakfast?"

"Because I'm a nice person who wants to buy you breakfast."

"You some kinda religious freak?"

"No, just someone who wants to buy you breakfast."

Both stared at each other, until Helen came to take an order.

"Do you want me to order for you?" Joyce asked.

"No. I'm not stupid. I can order my own breakfast."

Helen and Joyce exchanged glances. A confused Helen looked on.

"Pancakes," the girl finally spoke up. "With bacon."

"I'll have the same."

"And coffee," the girl added.

Joyce nodded to Helen. "Coffee for both of us."

"What's your name?" Joyce asked.

"What's yours?"

"Joyce."

"Amy."

"Hello Amy."

"Yeah, whatever. You work in this dump?"

"It's not a dump and yes, I work here. I make the pies."

"That sounds like a drag."

"It's better than what you do."

Joyce caught a blush of shock on the girl's face.

"Where do you live?" Joyce asked.

"Wherever."

"Is that Wherever, Arizona or Wherever, California?"

"So funny. None of your business, Joyce. Is this what I have to put up with for a free breakfast?"

"Yes, Amy, yes, it is. So, answer my questions?" Joyce said. "Where do you live and where is your family?"

"Got no family. I was with some foster parents in Yuma. Took off last month. I'm on my own."

Joyce froze. The words *foster parents* ringing in her ears.

"How old are you?"

"Sixteen."

"Amy, I'll ask again. How old are you?" she repeated.

With hesitancy she mumbled, "Fourteen. And don't even think about calling someone to send me back there. It'll take you and a small army to get me back to that shithole."

Joyce let out a long sigh and shook her head.

"I won't do that Amy. You want to know why I won't do that?"

"No, I don't want to know why you won't do that," Amy answered with dripping sarcasm.

"I was in foster care for eight years."

"Liar," Amy uttered.

"It wasn't horrible, bad, sometimes, but not horrible," Joyce continued, "Three families in eight years. The first two were just looking for a house cleaner and a full-time babysitter for the other kids and the monthly check. The third family was good. I communicated with them for years. They've since passed away. I liked them a lot, loved them even."

The food arrived and neither spoke for a while.

"But it's not really home. It's not like a real family. Is it, Amy?"

"I wouldn't know about that. My real family sucked. That's why I ended up in foster care. They're both in prison now, where they belong."

Joyce could only stare at this child.

Amy began to eat, quickly shoving the food in her mouth.

"Slow down, Amy. No one is going to take it away from you."

Amy looked up at Joyce and began to chew slower.

Joyce let her eat in silence.

"Would you like a slice of pie?" Joyce asked when they were done eating. "I made it this morning. I make the pies here."

"Yeah, so you said. Big deal," Amy muttered. "Do you have peach?"

"Yes, we have peach, made with fresh peaches that were picked yesterday morning."

"Okay."

Once the pie was eaten, Joyce asked Amy, "Where are you heading to, anyplace in particular? Are there relatives that you are trying to get to?"

"No. It's none of your business. I was just going. Not even knowing where. Just going. Maybe Phoenix. I don't know."

Joyce tapped her fork against her plate. A nervous habit that she picked up during her marriage.

"I have a nice little place not too far from here. You can stay there, until you figure out what you want to do."

Amy looked around the restaurant, at the fixtures, then at the other people. Joyce could see the fear and uncertainty in the young girl's eyes. A little girl was still there, a very frightened little girl.

She looked over at Joyce and nodded.

"You're not going to hold me there then report me to the cops or social workers."

"Amy, I already told you I won't do that."

"Why should I believe you?"

"Because there's another reason why I won't do that."

"Why?"

"Because I'm a runaway, just like you."

"Whadya talking about? You're full of it."

"It's a long story, but I do know how you feel. Believe me, I really do know how you feel. If someone tried to take me back to where I came from, I would run away again. Adults can be runaways too."

Amy said nothing.

"It's my secret. No one here knows that."

"Let's go," she added. "And don't steal anything on our way out."

Nothing was said by either of them on the way to Joyce's house. Joyce was trying to think of a story to tell her co-workers the next morning about this young girl that popped up out of nowhere.

Joyce showed her the spare room. It had a twin bed which was left behind by the previous tenant. She had put on new sheets and a bed-spread when she moved in, telling herself that it was silly. There would be no one visiting her, but Joyce couldn't stand a drab empty room and decorated it as if company were on its way. Now she was glad that she did.

Amy's eyes lit up when she saw the frilly room.

"I'll get you some towels," she said to Amy. "Take a shower. I have a robe you can wear until we figure out what we're going to do for your clothes. You are a tiny thing. You would swim in my things."

Amy, now compliant, just nodded. Joyce could see the weariness in her face and body as she headed for the bathroom.

Joyce was a realist and hid her purse before she headed for the back porch. As she did daily, she took in the sight of the valley below her.

What the hell have I done? She asked herself out loud. Joyce, you are something else, Leroy would say to her. She had to agree with him now.

When the sounds of the shower stopped, she met Amy outside the bathroom door with her terry cloth robe.

"Go lay down and take a nap. I have a feeling you haven't slept much lately. I'll wake you in a couple of hours and we'll go to Walmart and get you something to wear."

Amy sat on the bed and looked up at Joyce.

"Why are you doing this? You don't even know me."

Joyce shrugged.

"Because it needs to be done. I can't really explain it. You need help. I'm here to help. Take your nap. We'll talk later."

Without an argument the girl laid down and quickly fell asleep.

Joyce looked down at this child. The word *waif* came to her mind—an abandoned soul. What horrors has this child seen in her short life? She covered her with a quilt and prayed that she had good dreams.

During the trip to Wal Mart, Amy was quiet and subdued. She smiled at some of the choices Joyce made and accepted them without argument.

"We didn't get you a nightgown, but you can have one of my tee shirts," Joyce said after they got home and began to empty the bags.

"Thank you. I mean it. Thank you for doing this. I was a real bitch and you've been so nice," Amy said.

Joyce smiled and said, "No argument there. I don't know where this is heading, but in the meantime, there are ground rules."

Amy froze.

"Keep your room and this place clean. I hate clutter and mess."

"Okay."

"Okay," Joyce said.

"That's it?

"That's it. Now go change your clothes and I'll get something together for dinner."

Joyce had to smile when Amy walked in the room. The new clothes fit Amy perfectly and some of the purple faded from her hair, exposing her auburn hair. Without the makeup and in the new clothes she looked her age.

"You look cute, real cute."

"I kinda feel cute. Can't remember the last time I had new clothes."

"The dishes are in that cabinet. Set the table for dinner. Hope you like spaghetti and meatballs."

"I do."

"And salad."

"Okay," Amy said.

Then she smiled at Joyce—a pure smile, devoid of pretense.

Joyce's heart skipped a beat.

Joyce once again had to tell Amy to slow down when she was eating. Joyce understood that this was a result of having to share sparse meals and of not knowing when the next meal would come.

Later that evening, after the dishes were done, Joyce brought Amy a tee shirt to use as a night shirt.

"I go to sleep pretty early. I'm up at five every morning to get to the restaurant by six. I'm off by eleven, sometimes twelve. You can watch TV, just keep the volume down. I have basic cable so there aren't a lot of choices."

"That's okay."

"Amy."

"Yeah."

"You're welcome to stay as long as you want to. If you decide to leave, please let me know. I can't force you to stay here, but I also don't think it's a good idea to run off, unless you know where you're running off to."

"Can I ask you something?" she said to Joyce.

"Sure."

"Is there a husband or kids that are going to show up. They might not like this."

"Husband's dead. He died over six months ago. No kids, or relatives for that matter."

"Kinda like me," Amy replied. "Where you from?"

"I tell you what, Amy," Joyce replied. "I'll let you ask a question, but for every question you ask, I get to ask one in return."

"But not tonight," she added. "It's been a long day for both of us. But tomorrow, it will be question and answer time. Okay?"

"Uh huh."

"I'm off to bed. Good night, Amy."

"Good night, Joyce."

The next day, Joyce drove home not knowing if Amy would be there. She had left a note with her phone number and telling her to call if she needed anything. She hadn't heard a thing.

It was a relief when she walked in and she saw Amy on the sofa reading one of her paperbacks.

"Hi," Amy said. "Is it okay? I'm reading one of your books. Not much on TV."

"Of course. What did you pick?"

"*To Kill a Mockingbird*. I've heard about it and saw part of the movie once. It's kinda happy and sad, so far. But it's pretty good."

"I agree. There's a reason it's a classic."

"They were lucky that they had Atticus. He was a good father."

"Yes, they were."

"Makes me sad."

"Me too," Joyce replied. "What have you eaten today?"

"I had a bowl of cereal. I washed up when I was done."

"Thank you. I brought you a slice of pie."

"What kind?"

"Hope you like cherry."

"I do. Not a lot of food that I don't like."

"And I brought some tuna salad, so let's go have lunch."

It was in the middle of eating the pie that Joyce said, "So I get to ask a question."

"Huh?"

"Remember. You ask a question, then I ask a question. Okay?"

Amy shrugged.

"Are you really fourteen?" Joyce began

"Yes."

"Your turn," Joyce said.

"Where you from?" Amy asked.

"A small town in Wisconsin. Where are you from?"

"I was born in Phoenix. How old are you?"

"Forty-four. Where were you coming from yesterday morning?"

Joyce was hit with silence.

"Can you ask me something else?" Amy finally said.

"What's your last name?" Joyce asked.

"Sanderson. What's yours?" Amy responded.

"Oakley. Any brothers or sisters?" Joyce asked.

"Had a brother once. He died when I was little. That's kinda when my mother fell apart. What about you? Any brothers or sisters?"

"No. Only child. Parents died in a car accident when I was eight. Lived with some relatives for a while then ended up in foster care after that."

"Where was your foster home?" Joyce added.

Amy began to fidget.

Looking at Joyce with fear in her eyes, she asked "What if they come looking for me?"

"They won't find you. No one knows you're here. I even told the people at work that you're a visiting niece who's only going to be here a couple of days. They don't need to know more. And who are "they"?"

"Joyce. I don't want to do this no more."

"Another time, Amy. When you're ready? For now, let's go for a hike. It's something I do every afternoon, weather permitting. The views up here are great."

While they walked, Joyce looked over at Amy, who was wide-eyed as she looked around.

"It's so pretty. Wow!" Amy said.

"Yeah, it is. Sometimes it's just nice to walk and see what's around you."

"It's peaceful," Amy answered.

"How much school have you had, Amy?"

"Questions again?"

"Yep."

"Got through eighth grade. What about you? Were you a teacher?"

"No. Far from it. I was a cashier at a supermarket for years."

"You seem like a teacher."

"Really? I guess if things had been different, I might have gone to college and become a teacher. But I got married instead."

"How long were you married?"

"A long time. Did you like school?"

Amy shrugged. "I guess."

"I'm off tomorrow. We can drive over to the library. The closest one is thirty miles away. We'll get you some books. You need to keep up your education, no matter what happens in life."

"What if I don't stay?" Amy asked.

"Is that an official question?"

"No. What if you don't want me to stay? This gotta be a hassle for you. And expensive. I do have some money. I can pay you, like for room and board."

"Don't think like that. I don't want your money," she said. "Amy, we're both on some kind of a road. I'm not sure what's going on, other than you're a young girl in trouble. Let's just see what happens."

"Okay," Amy said softly.

"Okay."

That night, Joyce was awakened by a noise, a muffled scream. Confused at first, until she realized it was coming from Amy's room.

She found Amy, clutching at her blanket, breathing heavily, tears running down her cheeks.

Joyce ran over and held the girl, who offered no resistance. She told her to calm down. It was only a dream, she said to her, knowing that it was more than a dream.

"I'm sorry," Amy muttered. "I'm sorry."

Joyce wasn't sure if she was talking to her or to someone in the past.

"Don't be sorry. You have nothing to be sorry about. Now take a deep breath, go wash your face and I'll make us some hot chocolate."

Joyce knew from her own experience, after her parents died, that no one really wants to go back to sleep after a nightmare.

Joyce was at the stove when Amy walked in.

"I'm sorry I woke you up."

"Do you have them often?"

"The nightmares? Once in a while."

Joyce poured the hot chocolate.

"Amy, tell me about it."

"About what?"

"Your life. I'm not just being nosey. But I want to know what you've been through. I want you to feel that you can talk about it. Sometimes that helps. And I need to know more about you."

Amy said nothing and picked at the handle of her mug, long enough for Joyce to wonder if the girl would ever speak.

"After my brother died," she began softly. "my mother, well, she couldn't handle it. My father was in prison for armed robbery. She just had me and Dylan. When he died, she kinda went nuts. He got hit by a car. He was only six. She blamed herself. He was with her when he ran out in the street. She saw him get killed. After that she forgot about me. She got into drugs, then selling drugs and ended up in jail herself.

"My grandmother took me in but said she had her hands full with my grandfather who was sick. She called the social workers, and I went into foster care."

"How old were you?" Joyce asked softly.

"Eleven."

"Go on," Joyce prodded.

"It was this town like by the border of Arizona. The people were nice, and I went to school and it seemed okay. They said that they didn't have any other kids at home. Just a son who was out on his own.

"Well," she sighed, "one day this son came home. He lost his job and had no money and just moved back in. They fought all the time. He was mean to me. He didn't want me there. He was mean to them too. His name was Eugene. That's who I have the nightmares about sometimes. My first monster.

"Once, he told me to get him a beer from the refrigerator. I guess I didn't move fast enough, and he hit me. He told me to get my stuff and leave. I said no. He hit me again. I didn't know what to do. I liked his parents. I was there for over a year and it was okay. I didn't want to go and where would I go to? He threatened to really beat me if I told his parents what he did and said.

"I was afraid, but I stayed. I tried to stay out of his way as much as I could. But one night, one night..."

"Amy, what happened one night? It's okay. You're safe here."

"One night, it was real late. I was sleeping. He came in my room. He said since I wasn't leaving, I must be asking for it. Then he said if I would be nice to him, he would be nice to me."

She sighed before continuing. Her eyes darted around the room. Her hands began to tremble.

Joyce reached over and took her hands.

"He began to touch me. I couldn't get him to stop. It was horrible. He forced my legs apart. He covered my mouth and said I should shut the fuck up. He was busy. When he was done, he said he would scar me for life if I ever told anybody. A knife to my face he said. I'd look like a freak. Then he told me to get used to it. He would be back.

"It happened again a couple of nights later. The hard part was that I had to act like everything was normal in front of his parents. That was real hard. They were so nice. They didn't know that their son was a monster."

Now Joyce began to tremble. Amy became calm and detached.

"A couple of days later when they were all out of the house—they had to go to a funeral. I packed a few things, some food and water and some clothes. I left a note for his mom and dad thanking them. I stole some money from them, which I hated doing. They had a dresser draw where they kept some cash. I ran to town, where the bus station was and got on the next bus.

"I didn't even care where I was going. I went where I had enough money to go to. I was so scared of him. I wasn't going to let him do that to me again. It was so horrible.

"I ended up in San Diego, which was real pretty, and the weather was good. I hung out at the beach and slept on the streets and sometimes at shelters. I met other kids like me. We figured out ways to get money. It sounds crazy, but it was okay for a while, kinda fun. We looked out for each other."

She took a deep breath and would not make eye contact with Joyce.

"Then what happened Amy." Joyce asked softly.

"They came."

"Who came?"

"This woman and a couple of men. Her name was Bianca. One night I was in the park alone. It was stupid on my part. We were supposed to stick together, me and the other kids. It was getting dark out. Bianca made small talk with me. She actually asked me to walk her to the parking lot, that she was afraid to walk alone. When we got to the lot, two men showed up. They shoved me in the back of a truck. Bianca went in the back with me. She told me if I screamed, she would shoot me. She showed me the gun. Then she tied me up and taped my mouth. I didn't know where we ended up."

"You know what sex trafficking is, Joyce?"

No! No! No! screamed a voice in Joyce's head. Don't let this be. Not to this little girl! Please no!

"Yes, Amy, I do." She squeezed Amy's hand a bit harder.

"It's the most horrible, terrible thing. I wanted to die. I wished that they would kill me. All of those horrible men. I bet some of them had daughters. These horrible men tortured us. Then they left, satisfied and probably slept good that night. They all belong in the worst jail in the world. They all should have their dicks cut off. Without them, there would be no torturing kids. Filthy pigs."

"Oh, Amy. My God. You poor baby," Joyce's voice began to betray her horror at hearing this. "But you got away, Amy. You got away. Tell me. Tell me. How did you get away?"

"I set fire to the place. One of those fat old men dropped his cigarette lighter when he was done. I took it. Then I lit the filthy mattress on fire. I kinda didn't care if it killed me. When the flames got big, I started screaming fire. We all had to run out. That was the best time. I actually laughed when I saw all those scummy men running out trying to pull up their pants. Some didn't bother and came out with their bare butts. All us girls laughed when that building went up in flames.

"Waiting for the fire department to come, our owners tried to get us together, like cattle. We ran in different directions. I saw a pickup driving away and jumped in the back.

"I wasn't even sure what state I was in anymore. When he stopped for gas, I saw I was still in California. It was a truck stop in some small town. I figured that maybe I could get back to Phoenix. I wanted to visit my mother. I was going to go to the cops or a social worker or somebody and ask for help.

"I got out of the truck and ran. I didn't have any money, so I did the only thing I knew to get some. This was a truck stop. I did blowjobs for the bargain price of only thirty bucks. Then I started getting rides from these guys and that's how I ended up here. This last guy paid me the thirty and dropped me off here. He was going to Flagstaff to his wife and kids. Another filthy, pig.

"He said he'll look for me again. I was well worth it. Now there's something to be proud of, Joyce. I'm real good at blowjobs."

She finally looked up at Joyce.

"I can leave in the morning. I'm sure I disgust you. You're like this decent good person and I'm a fourteen-year-old whore. I have a little bit of money, so I'll get by for a while."

"Oh my God, Amy no. Not at all. Not at all. You don't disgust me. Far from it. You're brave and you're tough, and good. People did this to you. No, you're not going anywhere. You're going to stay right here with me."

Amy's body began to shake. The shaking with sobs that came with release. Joyce took her in her arms. Amy hugged her back. They wept together.

"I'll protect you, Amy. I promise. I promise. You never have to do that again."

Joyce stayed with Amy when they went back to bed. She lay with Amy in her arms until the girl fell asleep. Only then did she go back to her room.

The next morning, they both slept in late. Joyce asked Amy if she'd like to go out for breakfast.

"McDonalds?" she replied.

"If that's your idea of going out for breakfast, then we will go to McDonalds. And then we go to the library. Deal?"

"Deal."

Amy insisted on paying for both breakfasts.

"I told you I had a little bit of money," Amy said, after Joyce looked at her with a raised eyebrow.

After breakfast, they headed over to the library, where Joyce found a number of books, not just novels, but some history and geography books that she felt would be good for Amy to study.

"That's a lot of books," Amy said when she saw the pile.

"You've missed a lot of school. We'll go through them together. I'm not even sure what I'll remember. It'll be our version of home schooling."

"Hmm, sounds like a good time, Joyce."

"It'll be a riotous good time, Amy."

"Can we stop at a Walgreens or a drug store. I need some stuff."

Amy filled up a basket with some personal items, as well as magazines and candy.

When they got in the car, she looked over at Joyce.

"I need to get rid of this money. It makes me sick to look at it. I know where it came from. It even smells bad."

A strange but understandable reaction. Joyce thought.

"Tell you what. Give it to me. I'll take it to the bank and exchange it for new bills. If you want, maybe we can open a little savings account that you'll have access to."

"Geez, Joyce. You are something else. You have an answer for everything."

"You sound like my late husband. He always said that. That I was something else."

"Joyce?"

"Amy."

"You said you were a runaway. What were you running from? Hope it's a better story than mine."

"My husband was a lousy husband. He didn't beat me or anything. I wasn't really anything to him. I cooked and cleaned and made him his favorite pies. I dealt with all day-to-day problems. I was more of a care-taker then a wife. He couldn't have lasted a month without me. I felt like he was my job not my husband. But that was the way he wanted it and that's the way it was. That's what I signed up for when I married him.

"He dropped dead from a heart attack at work. He was a mechanic. A couple of days after the funeral, I packed a few things, lit some candles, turned on the burners of the stove, got in the car and drove away. I was on the road when I heard the explosion. To be perfectly honest, it was a good feeling."

"You blew up your own house! Damn, Joyce, you're a bad ass! A real bad ass. Did you ever see those action movies? That's like you. Driving away with like explosions in the background. Wow. I'm impressed."

"Don't be. It was reckless and I could have hurt or even killed someone."

"You sure you didn't?"

"I checked on the library internet. There was an article about it in a couple of papers and everyone is still looking for me, especially the cops. No one got hurt. They thought I was in there at first and then figured it out. I do believe it's a crime to blow up a house, even if it's your own."

"So, you're a fugitive from justice?"

"Yeah," she said with a smile. "I guess I am."

"Well, don't worry. I got your back, Joyce."

"Thanks, Amy. I got your back too."

They fell into a comfortable routine. Joyce going to work. Amy cleaning the house then going through the books. Joyce added to the collection from purchases made at garage sales. Amy absorbed what she could, but there was much of it she didn't understand. It was times like this when she wished she were in school with a teacher.

Joyce explained what she could, but it became obvious to Joyce that it was time for a computer.

Leroy had a computer at the repair shop and didn't feel the need for one at home. Too expensive, he would claim. Joyce knew he meant that he wouldn't know how to operate one. Her experience with computers were, like Leroy, limited to their jobs.

She saw no need for one in her new life. There were no friends or relatives to email. Nothing that she couldn't find out on television or in the daily paper. She simply didn't see the need for one, until now.

So, Joyce went computer shopping and signed up for the Internet.

Amy had some experience with computers when she did go to school, but Joyce ended up taking classes at the library. In time they both became quite proficient.

"Joyce," Amy asked one day. "Did you know you can find prison records on this thing?"

"What are you saying? You want to look up your parents?"

"Yeah."

"Go ahead," Joyce said, pulling up a chair next to the girl.

It wasn't long before a picture of a woman, a sickly, dark eyed woman popped up on the screen.

"Mom?" Joyce asked.

"Mom," she replied. "Still another year for her to go."

"Do you want to visit her? The prison is about a four- or five-hour drive from here. It's something we can do if you want to. We can stay overnight somewhere—a road trip."

"Yeah, that sounds good. I think I'll write first. Maybe she'll write back. Can I give her your number? Maybe she'll call."

"That's fine with me."

A letter went out that day with Joyce's address and phone number.

She didn't bother with her father.

It was three weeks later, when Joyce came home from work, that she saw Amy sitting on the sofa staring straight ahead, a letter clasped in her hand. She mutely handed it over to Joyce.

The letter was from the warden at the prison, apologizing that she had to inform Amy of the death of her mother, six months earlier. It was an accident in the laundry. Amy's mom had fallen and severely hit her head. She never regained consciousness and died in a coma. They also apologized that they couldn't inform her sooner, but they had no way of reaching Amy.

"Oh no, Amy," Joyce said as she put her arm around the girl. "I am so terribly sorry. So very sorry."

Amy shrugged.

"I hardly knew her. Ya know. I'm not even sure I remember what she looked like. I wish I had a picture of her. I know she was pretty. She had a good laugh. She was funny. That was before she went bad, ya know."

"Maybe we can find out what they did with her belongings. I'll check into it. They must have sent them to someone."

"Yeah, whatever. I'm going for a walk. No studying today, Joyce."

It was after several days of Amy moving zombie-like around the house, the house and the books ignored, when Joyce made a suggestion."

"I'm really busy at the restaurant. I could use some help. Flo hasn't been feeling so hot and I'm starting to go crazy keeping up. You think you'd like to give me a hand. I'd really appreciate it."

"What do I know about making pies?"

"I'll teach you. But right now, I just need help with things like cutting up the fruit and some prep work and of course, the cleanup. You'll get paid. And it'll get you out of the house."

"What about Flo and what's his name? Will they let you do that?"

"Yes, they don't want to lose me and if I don't get some help, they will. At least until September."

"What's September?"

"That's when they'll be expecting you to go to school. Right now, all they know is that my niece is staying with me."

"So, what do we say in September?"

"We'll cross that bridge when we reach it."

"Yeah, I guess. Whatever," Amy replied, almost inaudible.

"Amy, you need to get out of the house," Joyce said. "You need to see other people. I'm like the only person you have any contact with. It's time to get out."

Joyce could see the rage surfacing—an explosion was imminent. The girl's hands were trembling, her face reddening.

"And what do I talk about with other people, Joyce!" she said, her voice now piercing the room. "What it's like to fuck ten to fifteen men in one day? How to give a good blowjob? How about my parents? We can talk about my dead mother who was in jail for dealing drugs, and my criminal bank robbing father. What Joyce? What do I say to people? To normal people in normal families with normal kids. What the fuck do I say to anyone—ever!"

"Amy, you make up shit!" Joyce said even louder. "That's what you do. What do you think I do and have done since I moved here? I tell them what a great husband I had and about all my friends and relatives in Wisconsin. I don't mention that I blew up my house and took off or that I hated everyone in that miserable little town and that I don't have a single friend or relative that gives a shit about me.

"You learn how to make up a life and stick to it. Mostly, you avoid personal questions and just keep asking them things. Most people like to talk about themselves anyway and don't remember what you told them. Someone asks you a question you don't want to answer, you change the subject.

Joyce could see that she diffused the tension in the girl.

Amy, for the first time in days smiled.

"Joyce, yeah, right," she said, "Good, A great life lesson you're giving this teenager. Lie your ass off. Just make up shit. Bull shit everybody. You're a great role model, Joyce."

It started as a giggle from Joyce and became crazed, laughter that buckled both of them over.

"You sure I can't tell them how to give a good blowjob?" Amy said when she caught her breath.

"Maybe I should tell them how to blow up a house?"

They laughed until they could laugh no more.

After a good hug, Amy agreed to work at the bakery, but told Joyce to be ready to put up with the complaining about the early hours.

Their lives now revolved around new routines for both of them. Baking in the morning, studying and reading in the afternoon, hiking in the evenings. Joyce's co-workers commented on how nice her niece was, quiet but nice, not a smart-mouth teenager that you see so often these days or the ones whose noses were always in their cellphones.

Cellphone, Joyce thought. *I should get her a cellphone. Even a cheap one so that she could call me if something came up, for emergencies. The time will come when she's not always at my side. Hopefully, the time will come when she develops friendships with kids her age.*

She put it on her list, alongside school, a driver's license, winter clothes, pictures of Amy's mother. Things that she would have to take care of, but where do you begin when you aren't a parent or even a legal guardian. How do I file for anything when I don't want anyone checking into my past? Even the view from her back porch couldn't stop the heart palpitations that happened when these thoughts crept in. She wished she had someone to ask, a good friend to confide in. Loneliness crept in at times like this, but solutions didn't.

But I can get her a cellphone. I'll upgrade mine and get a new one for her. She'll be thrilled.

It was another hot morning for Joyce. Summer was in full swing. Temperatures in the hundreds in Phoenix, the nineties up here. She was at her place at the picnic table with her cup of coffee and her notepad. Spending time around an oven this time of year was brutal. She tried to stick to refrigerator pies, but there was no escaping the oven. The crusts still had to be baked and people still asked for apple and peach pies.

She had sent Amy home early. No reason to subject her to this heat. It was over a two mile walk back to the house, but Amy didn't mind. She had all the makings of a good hiker.

Joyce looked up from her list at the lot across the road. The same lot and the same road where she first saw Amy. And now the same white truck pulled into the lot. Amy's words reverberated in her head.

"He said he'll look for me again. I was well worth it."

Joyce's heart skipped a beat. She wrote something on her notepad.

He got out of the truck and was heading her way.

He was young, probably in his thirties, with the makings a beer belly—unshaven and grimy.

Joyce smiled at him.

"Hi there," she said, bile gathering in her throat.

"Hey, how ya doin? The food any good here?"

"The food is great here. Especially the pies. I make them."

"That right?"

"Looks like you've been on the road a while."

"Yeah, just got in from California. Did eight hours straight."

"What brings you to our little town?" Joyce asked. "We don't get too many trucks up here. Don't suppose you just happened to hear about the pies?"

"Nah," he said with a snigger. "Took a little side trip."

Joyce nodded, hoping he would say more, and he did.

"Actually, I'm looking for a friend of mine, well, the niece of a friend. He said I should look her up and see how she's doing."

"Now who would that be?"

She dug her pen into her notepad.

"Her name is Amy. About sixteen, seventeen, Long hair, brown but you never know with girls. Could be purple or whatever."

"I know who you mean."

"Ya do?"

"Yeah. Nice kid, real quiet. Purple hair."

"Yeah, that's probably her. Where can I find her?" he asked while scratching his inner thigh.

"Tell you what. I'll give you the directions to her aunt's place. Not far from here. You go in and get something to eat. You look like you can use a good meal. Order a piece of pie. I'll be right in."

"Sounds good. First I need to use the john and wash up some."

"So, what's your name?" she asked.

"Roy." He held his hand out for a shake. "And you?"

"Joyce. Pleased to meet you Roy," she said as she shook his hand. "I'll meet you inside."

She followed him as she did Amy on that day. He headed for the men's room.

She wrote down the directions to her house. When she saw him get settled in a booth she walked over and gave him the paper.

"Have a good visit, Roy. I'm sure she'll be glad to see you. She's a sweet kid."

"Yeah, she is."

She called Amy on her way out the door.

"Are you home yet?" she asked sounding more frantic than she wanted to sound.

"Yeah. Just walked in. Why?"

"I'll be home in a little bit, and I'll explain. Just stay put. Don't leave the house, for nothing. And don't open the door. Understand?"

"Okay. But you're kinda scaring me."

Joyce hung up, ran to her car and sped off.

"Amy," she said as she walked in the house. "Amy, was his name Roy?"

"What? Who?"

"The man in the truck. The white truck that brought you here. Was his name Roy?"

Amy paled.

"He, he, he said it was. Is he here? Is he looking for me? He said he would Joyce, he said he would. Oh no. Oh God."

A wide-eyed look and the sudden shudders overtook the girl.

"Amy, I need you to keep it together. You understand. He is not going to hurt you. Remember when you said I always have an answer for everything?"

"Yeah," she responded. "But I'm afraid. I'm afraid. What if he finds me Joyce? What if he finds me when you're not here?"

"Amy, listen to me," Joyce ordered.

She grabbed her by the shoulders.

"He is coming here."

"What! No, Joyce, Call the cops, do something. I don't want to do that no more."

"Amy, calm down and just listen to me. When he gets here. I want you to answer the door. I'll be right behind you, behind the door, listening. I'll take it from there."

Joyce went into her bedroom, reached under her bed and pulled out a shotgun.

Amy's stared openmouthed when Joyce walked into the room with it.

"I told you I'll take care of it. It's the one thing that Leroy owned that I took before I left. It can be a scary thing—a woman alone on the open road."

Amy said nothing, sat on the sofa and clasped her shaking hands together.

It wasn't long before they heard the truck pull up in the driveway. Next came the sound of the truck door closing, heavy footsteps on the front porch and a knock on the door.

Joyce stood behind the door as Amy answered it.

"Hey Amy," he said. "It's me Roy. We met a couple of months ago. I said I'd look you up when I'm in the area."

She nodded.

"Hi, Roy, Yeah, I remember you."

"Feel like going for a drive?"

Joyce slowly appeared in Amy's place. Shotgun in her arms.

"The girl's not going anywhere."

A stunned Roy gawked at Joyce.

"Number one. The girl is fourteen years old, you filthy rapist," she said evenly. "Number two. I have your license plate and employer's name and number from your truck. I'm sure your employer will be very interested in what you're doing when not delivering whatever kind of shit you deliver."

"Three. I'm sure I can track down your wife in Flagstaff. She'll be interested as well."

"And finally, if you ever come near this girl or any other young girl and I find out, I will not hesitate to shoot you between your filthy, scummy legs."

"Now, let's just calm down, Joyce," Roy said. "She told me she was eighteen and asked me if I wanted to party."

"Shut up you disgusting pig. Because you see, I am dying to pull the trigger and tell the cops that I came home and found you raping my niece here."

"Alright, alright, stupid bitch. Put that damn thing away. Get a grip for Christ sake."

He put his hands up and began to walk backwards.

"And she'll do it too. You pig!" An emboldened Amy yelled from behind Joyce. "She blew her own house up, cuz she was pissed. She won't hesitate to shoot you."

"And spread the word with your other disgusting perverts to stop fucking young girls," Joyce added. "Like I said, I'm dying to pull this trigger."

"Okay, fuck, Okay. I'm going," he said. "And don't be telling no one. I'm not a bad guy."

Joyce took a shot up in the air hitting the tree in front of the house and scattering a cascade of branches and leaves.

Roy hit the dirt and covered his head.

Joyce went over and kicked him in his waist.

"Get in your truck and get the hell out of here. I better not ever see you around here again."

"Fine. Fine. Crazy, fucking lunatic," he said as he fumbled for his keys.

Amy stood behind Joyce and they watched as he drove away.

"Damn, Joyce. You really are a bad ass."

"I told you, Amy, I have your back."

"You sure do, Joyce. You sure do."

"Joyce?"

"Amy."

"Love you."

"Love you too."

Here I Am

Tom, hurry up. I don't want you to miss your flight,
and it's on time.

Here I am. All packed and ready to go.

Ken's here to drive you to the airport.

I'm really nervous about this.
I think I'm in over my head.

It'll be fine. You are so talented.
You'll do great.

This is LA. I've never even been out
of this state. Much less auditioning in LA.

Tom, they asked for you after seeing
your performance here.

Yeah, I know.
I wish you were coming with. I'd be braver.

Me too. But that's not going to happen.
And you'll have a great time without me.
I'll be getting all the news I need on the weather
channel. It's a beautiful 78 degrees
over there today.

I'm probably overdressed.
I mean it's 38 degrees out here today.
Hard to believe it can be 78 over there.

I know. And I know that you're really
eager to go now, so go.

You okay?

I'm fine. I'll miss you, so make sure you call,
and call often. It's not like I'm busy.
Remember. Just be yourself.
Let your sincerity and honesty shine through.

Yeah, Okay. I'll miss you too.

I'll be with you. Even though I'm far away.

I know. Love you, Dad.

Love you too, Son.

Simon watched from the window as his son got into the car. They waved at each other as the car pulled away. The love for his only child mixed with envy.

Once the car was out of sight, he wheeled his chair to the kitchen and poured himself another coffee. His cat Lulu jumped on his lap as she often did when he wasn't moving.

"It's just you and me now, Lulu old girl," he said as he stroked her back. The sound of her purring the only noise in the room.

He fought the urge to get sentimental. Sentimentality usually brought on sadness. This was no time to be sad. It was a time to be overjoyed and proud. His son was embarking on a new career. He had been contacted by an agent and a producer after the rave reviews of his performance on stage this past summer.

He would make it and he would make it big. Simon had no doubt about that.

He checked the time. His caregiver would be there soon. That meant a shower, a shave, and clean clothes. At the beginning, he balked at the idea of a caregiver. Initially, Simon hated those visits—the humiliation, the helplessness, his useless, unworkable body. But things changed. Now, he looked forward to the visits. The conversations with the caregivers—that was what he enjoyed the most. The human interaction with someone beside the usual few friends who stopped in on occasion. The details of someone else's lives besides his own remained with him after they left.

As always thoughts of his late wife surfaced.

She would be so proud, he thought. *Jenna, sweet Jenna. So talented. What a voice. It was Jenna that brought Tom into the world of acting and singing, while he worked at his printing company. Tom took to it at such an early age. Yes, she would be thrilled. He'll be living her dream.*

The unceasing reminder of the accident that killed her and left him in a wheelchair unable to do many of the everyday fundamental acts seared through his brain as it always did. Every pleasant memory was always woven with torment and reality.

He looked up at the clock and smiled. Today was Tuesday. Today was the day that Gina would come. Gina with the light brown hair, the flawless face, the perfect figure. So young, so beautiful. He couldn't understand what she was doing as a caregiver. *There's a big, beautiful world out there,* he wanted to shout at her. *Why do you spend it tending to my wasted useless body? You should be traveling the world. You should be spending your days with other beautiful people on the beaches of southern France. Or walking down Fifth Avenue in New York.*

That's when his fantasies would overtake him.

In his mind he became a handsome, healthy fifty plus widower with a celebrity son. In his mind he would be in New York after seeing his son perform on Broadway. Of course, Gina would be on his arm, smiling—radiant with that look women have when in the crosshairs of love.

In his mind they would be dining at one of the many elegant restaurants that dotted the city. Of course, they would be joined by Tom and his celebrity friends. Despite the age difference, Gina would have no interest in them other than their fascinating conversations. Deep down, she wanted the security of a good man, a good marriage. Of course, there would be no children. Her focus would be on him only.

Instead of cleaning his body, she would be caressing it. Instead of tending to it, she would be enjoying it.

Of course, there will be money. After he sold the house and the business there would be enough money to maintain this lifestyle. He was a smart businessman and did well financially.

They would be happy. His mind carried him to a small club, where they would dance—slowly, intimately, oblivious to others in the club and the world.

Then they would return to their apartment that overlooked Central Park. After a nightcap, they would go to the bedroom and make love for as long as their bodies allowed.

In the morning they would make plans for a European trip—the wheres and the whens.

He would be living.

The squawk of the doorbell caused him to shudder back to reality.

He moved as quickly as his chair would allow to open the door.

And there stood Gina, in her crinkled scrubs, with hair that fell from her ponytail draping her smiling face.

The sight of her forced Simon to sit up as straight as his body would allow and smile back at her.

I can make it through another day, he thought. *I can make it through another day.*